Tentatively, Camille touched his arm. "Michael? Is something wrong?"

"Yes."

She waited for him to elaborate, and when it became obvious he wasn't going to, said, "Can you tell me about it?"

When at last he turned to her, his eyes were so empty she might have been looking at a dead man. She had no idea whether he was angry, or ill, or just very tired.

"No. You're the last person I can talk to," he said.

"Why?"

He inhaled deeply. "I have no business being here with you tonight—no right at all cultivating an acquaintance with you."

"Because we come from different worlds?"

He let out a bark of laughter. "More than you can begin to imagine."

Catherine Spencer, once an English teacher, fell into writing through eavesdropping on a conversation about Mills & Boon® romances. Within two months she changed careers, and sold her first book to Mills & Boon in 1984. She moved to Canada from England forty years ago and lives in Vancouver. She is married to a Canadian and has four grown children—two daughters and two sons—plus two dogs and a cat. In her spare time she plays the piano, collects antiques and grows tropical shrubs.

Recent titles by the same author:

THE PREGNANT BRIDE
MISTRESS ON HIS TERMS
THE MILLIONAIRE'S MARRIAGE

D'ALESSANDRO'S CHILD

BY

CATHERINE SPENCER

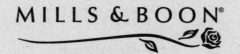

First published in Great Britain 2001
Harlequin Mills & Boon Limited,
Eton House, 18-24 Paradise Road, Richmond, Surrey TW9 1SR

© Kathy Garner 2001

ISBN 0 263 82571 X

Set in Times Roman 10½ on 12 pt.
01-0202-52057

Printed and bound in Spain
by Litografia Rosés, S.A., Barcelona

CHAPTER ONE

INITIALLY, all Mike planned to do was observe the child. From a distance. To establish, as well as he could, that all was well in the boy's life. That done, he would pay a last visit to his dying ex-wife, ease her tortured mind and heart, then take the first flight out of San Francisco and head back to Vancouver without disclosing to another living soul that, more than four years earlier, she'd conceived a child. Mike would even try to forget it.

It seemed the most decent thing to do; the most humane. Because enough damage had already occurred, and what right had he to plow into matters at this late stage and make them worse?

But that was before. Before he could put a face to the child. Before he heard the infectious belly laugh of delight, or saw the dark hair so much like his own, or watched the sturdy, sun-kissed legs pumping across the grassy slope to the carousel at the other side of the park.

After that, *observing from a distance* just wasn't enough. He wanted to touch. To speak, to listen. To learn everything about the three and a half years since this child, this son he hadn't known he'd sired, had come into the world— little things like what foods he preferred, what his favorite toy was, if he liked music, or model trains; whether or not he could kick a ball, skate, swim.

A few yards from where he watched, the woman—the "mother"—waved to the boy as he swirled past on a painted pony. "Hold on tight, sweetheart," she called out, her voice as musical as a genteel bell.

Hold on tight! The words held a bitter irony for Mike. Perhaps if he and Kay had held on tight to their marriage, he wouldn't be here now, trying to devise a way to strike up a conversation without raising suspicion.

Already he felt people were watching him, wondering about the stranger in their midst. In a town as small and seriously upscale as this, a guy in blue jeans stood out from the crowd as plainly as his midsize rental car looked out of place snugged up between the Mercedes and BMWs in the tree-shaded parking area.

The merry-go-round wound to a stop with the boy on the side farthest away from his mother. Standing on tiptoe, the skirt of her pretty mauve dress billowing slightly in the breeze, she waved to catch his attention. ''Over here, Jeremy!''

Jeremy? He'd come across worse names, Mike supposed, but this one was a bit on the arty side for his taste. A boy needed a name that would sit easily on him when he grew to be a man. Something strong and indisputedly masculine. Like *Michael.* And a last name that reflected his heritage. Like *D'Alessandro.*

Slithering off his pony, the boy raced around the carousel and in his eagerness to get back to his mother, tripped and went sprawling practically at Mike's feet. Without stopping to consider the wisdom of such a move, Mike stooped to haul the little guy upright again.

There were grass stains on his knees. And the faint remains of baby dimples. The little body was sweetly solid, the eyes staring into his the same dark, fathomless brown as Kay's.

The feelings...sheesh, how to describe them! It was as if a hollow suddenly opened up inside Mike; a sense of loss so acute that he caught his breath at the pain of it. The child fearfully shying away from him was his own flesh and blood!

He ached to reassure him. To cup the smooth round cheek in his callused hand, to hug the innocent little body close and just once whisper, *You don't have to be afraid of me, son. I'm your daddy.*

Instead, he mumbled, ''Hey, sport,'' then dribbled into awkward silence because, while he never had to think twice about what to say to his four-year-old twin nephews, with *this* child he had to watch his words.

A shadow slid across the grass, just wide enough to block out the sun. ''Come here, Jeremy.''

Even lightly coated with alarm, her voice remained musical and lovely. The hand which reached down to pluck her child out of a stranger's grasp was narrow and elegant, with long slender fingers and delicate oval nails painted pink.

Glancing up, Mike found himself pinned in a wary silver-blue gaze rimmed with feathery lashes. Straightening, he took a step backward and said casually, ''He took quite a nosedive, but I don't think he's hurt.''

She was too well-bred to tell him she no more gave a flying fig what he thought than she appreciated his touching her child, but the message came across clearly enough in her cool reply. ''I'm sure he isn't, but thank you for being concerned. Jeremy, say thank you to the gentleman for being kind enough to help you.''

''Thank you,'' Jeremy parroted, inspecting him with the uninhibited curiosity of any normal three-year-old now that he had the safety of his mother's leg to cling to.

Mike wished he dared ruffle that thick mop of black hair—just once experience the pleasure of its texture slipping through his fingers. But it was out of the question. *She* was watching him too intently, her protective instincts on full alert. So hooking his thumbs in the back pockets of his jeans and hoping his grin didn't look too manufactured, he settled for, "Any time, kiddo."

"Well...." The mother folded the boy's hand protectively in her own and turned away. "We must be going. Thank you again."

"Sure thing."

He watched them leave, her with the erect carriage of a duchess, and his boy with the agile enthusiasm that only the very young and innocent could know. *You've accomplished what you came to do,* Mike's rational mind informed him. *The child's well-dressed, well-fed, and well-mannered, and even a fool can see the mother dotes on him. Convey the news to Kay, then stick to your original idea and forget this afternoon ever happened.*

"Fat chance," he murmured, his gaze trained on the pair as they joined the lineup at the buffet tables set out under striped, open-sided tents.

The scene, perfect down to the last detail, might have been lifted from a painting. Too bad it couldn't erase the picture indelibly imprinted on his mind of the room in St. Mary's Hospital in San Francisco, and Kay's face, already pared by illness to skeletal proportions, rendered even more pitiful by her mental anguish.

"I gave him away," she'd whispered, her sunken eyes filling with tears and her fingers, so bony they resembled claws, worrying the hospital sheet stretched across her painfully thin body. "Finding I was pregnant, just when I was starting out afresh...with such ambitions. I was so close to achieving my dream...I could smell the success. I couldn't handle a baby, Mike. Not then."

But I could have, he thought bitterly. The brief taste he'd just enjoyed told him that, and he was ravenous suddenly, not for the food people were heaping on their plates, but for closer acquaintance with a child who should have belonged to him.

He could no more walk away and forget the boy existed than a starving man could refuse nourishment.

"Who's your secret admirer, Camille?"

Though lightly phrased and threaded with amusement, the question brought a flush to Camille's cheeks which completely undercut her offhand, "I haven't the foggiest idea what you mean."

"Oh, come off it! This is *me* you're talking to!"

She should have known better than to try fooling the woman who'd been her best friend since kindergarten. Frances Knowlton hadn't shared her secret passion for Mortimer Griffin at nine, helped her dye her naturally blond hair a horrific ruby red at fifteen, supported her at twenty through a wedding involving four hundred guests, and kept her together when her marriage fell apart the year she turned twenty-eight, without learning a thing or two along the way.

"If you're referring to the man at the table over there," she said, refusing to glance his way even though her eyes would have been happy to feast on him indefinitely if she'd allowed it, "we met very casually over by the carousel. He was kind to Jeremy."

"Which no doubt explains why you're practically drooling at the mere mention of him now. Not that I blame you." Fran, never one to care too much about social protocol, lowered her sunglasses and subjected the stranger to a frank inspection before fondling her husband's knee under the table. "If I weren't already happily married to the sexiest man on earth, I'd be sticking a Sold sign on Mr. Blue Eyes' forehead before anyone else, including you, Camille, beat me to it."

He did have the most gorgeous eyes, Camille was forced to admit. Not the pale blue-gray she'd been cursed with, but a deep, tropical indigo that blazed with an almost electric energy from his tanned face. And he did keep switching that gaze to her. She could feel it pulsing across the distance between them, a magnet persistently drawing her attention away from Jeremy who was up to his elbows in crabmeat salad.

"Isn't it a shame that, like you, he's here alone?" Fran observed, flinging down her paper napkin and swinging her long legs over the picnic bench. "In the spirit of small town hospitality, I think I should do something about that."

Heat rushed into Camille's face again. "Please don't, Fran! For a start, I'm not alone, I'm with Jeremy, and...."

But she might as well have saved her breath. Fran had already descended with single-minded determination on the man seated two tables away. He was acknowledging whatever she said to him, his initial look of inquiry giving way to a dazzling smile.

A moment later, he'd scooped up his plate and was loping behind her as she wove her way back to where Camille sat stony-faced with embarrassment.

"If I were you, I'd try to keep my wife under better control," she informed Adam Knowlton.

Adam grinned. "Short of keeping her on a very short leash and muzzling her, there's not much I can do. She's her own woman, always has been, and I wouldn't have her any other way." Then, as Fran made a beeline for a seat next to her husband, thereby leaving the stranger with no choice but to sit beside Camille, Adam leaned forward and muttered, "Better take the scowl off your face and smile, sweet thing. You're about to be introduced."

His name was Michael D'Alessandro. He was, he said, on a working vacation. He lived north of the border, in

Vancouver, and owned a construction company and was chiefly interested in building town houses. Back home, the Californian style of architecture was very popular, and he'd come south in part to solicit bids for designs on a gated community he hoped to develop on a tract of land he'd recently acquired.

He said a lot of other things, too: that he couldn't believe his luck in running into Adam who was an architect specializing in earthquake-proof residential construction; that he'd discovered Calder by chance and found it very picturesque.

He answered Fran's not-so-subtle questions with forthright charm. Married? Not anymore. Traveling alone? Yes. Just passing through or planning to stay in town awhile? No fixed time frame; he was his own boss and could pretty much do as he pleased.

He even found time to pay attention to Jeremy, drawing him out with the ease of someone used to being around small children. Jeremy responded like a starving plant to water, bursting into infectious giggles and showing off with three-year-old pride. "I can swim," he announced. "And I've got a football and I got my hair cut," all of which information Michael D'Alessandro received with absorbed attention.

But the only thing that really registered with Camille was the instinctive feeling that everything about the man spelled trouble, from his mesmerizing, take-no-prisoners eyes, to his stunning smile and his sexy, come-hither voice.

Sexy? She almost fell off the bench in astonishment. How had *sexy* managed to sneak into her thoughts? She must have a touch of sunstroke! "Sexy" was no more a part of her vocabulary these days than "romance." She'd renounced both and concentrated all her love and passion on Jeremy ever since the day her marriage fell apart and Todd walked out not just on her, but on their child as well.

"So what's this public picnic all about, or do people in Calder always get together for a crabfest on summer weekends?"

Fran kicked her under the table, alerting Camille to the fact that the sexy voice had finally got around to addressing a direct question at her. Flustered, she avoided meeting his gaze and stared instead at his hands.

He had a working man's hands, big and tanned and capable. Like his arms and, no doubt, all the rest of him so snugly encased in white T-shirt and blue jeans softened to doeskin by numerous washings. Nothing like Todd, who turned a fiery red if he stayed out in the sun very long, and who thought muscle sat best on those who didn't have much in the brain department.

"Tell Michael about the women's shelter, Camille," Fran prompted, in much the same tone of voice one might use with a social incompetent suddenly turned loose in public.

"Women's shelter?" As he shifted to look at her more fully, Michael D'Alessandro's arm brushed against Camille's. If finding herself the focus of those arresting blue eyes wasn't disturbing enough, the shock of his actually touching her ran clean past her shoulder and settled somewhere in the vicinity of her throat, temporarily impairing her vocal cords—not to mention her mental faculties.

"I...." she croaked, shredding a corner of her paper napkin. "We—a group of us, that is...it's a project we thought was...um, worthwhile."

"As usual, she's being too modest," Fran chimed in, rolling her eyes in exasperation when Camille stumbled into silence. "She's chair of the fund-raising committee—

is the one who started the ball rolling in the first place, come to that, and it's mostly thanks to her efforts that it's been so successful.''

Camille swallowed, and vowed she'd throttle Fran the very first chance she got.

''Is that so?'' Laugh lines creased the corners of his eyes as he let loose with a smile that could have melted the polar ice cap. ''I wouldn't have expected there'd be a need for such a place in a town like this.''

''There isn't. It's in San Francisco,'' she said baldly.

''I see.'' A shadow of sadness seemed to cross his face and he lowered his eyes briefly. He had ridiculously long lashes. And sleek level brows as black as his hair which needed a trim. An inch longer and the ends would touch the crew neck of his T-shirt.

Aware she was staring, Camille turned her attention to Jeremy on her other side, glad that the conversation seemed to have petered out.

Fran, though, wasn't about to let that happen. ''If you're interested in supporting the cause, you're welcome to buy a ticket to our annual gala next Saturday,'' she informed the man breezily. ''You'll get a fabulous evening's entertainment in return—gourmet catering, live dance music, fabulous door prizes—and the really good part is, it's all tax deductible.''

''Not for Mr. D'Alessandro,'' Camille put in quickly. ''He's not a U.S. resident. In any case, I doubt he'd be interested in attending a function where he doesn't know anyone.''

''I know you,'' Michael D'Alessandro said, bathing her in another sultry smile. ''Not well, perhaps, but enough that I'd like to know you better.''

Fran jumped on that faster than a flea on a well-fed dog. ''Well, isn't it amazing how things work out sometimes!

Would you believe that, less than an hour ago, Camille told me she hasn't yet lined herself up with an escort? You'd be doing her a double favor if you bought a ticket and offered your services.''

''Fran, honestly!'' Truly annoyed, Camille turned a scathing glare on her friend. ''I don't need you to set me up with a man, and I'm quite sure Mr. D'Alessandro doesn't appreciate being pressured like this. Drop the subject, please.''

''I don't feel pressured,'' he said mildly. ''Surprised, perhaps. I'd have thought your husband would be your date.''

''I don't have a husband. My marriage broke up two years ago.''

For some reason, the news rendered him temporarily speechless. She couldn't imagine why. People got divorced all the time, as he should know. She was hardly unique.

He soon recovered, though. ''In that case,'' he said, ''I'd be honored to act as your escort.''

''I can't allow it. For a start, you're on vacation and might have other plans for next Saturday.''

''As a matter of fact, I don't, at least not in the evening. So unless you're afraid I'll step all over your feet—''

''It's not that!''

He regarded her quizzically. ''Then what is it?''

''Everything!'' She shook her head, bewildered by her agitation. ''Even discounting the fact that we've barely met, I haven't been part of the singles scene in over ten years.''

''Perhaps,'' he suggested gravely, ''it's time you got used to the idea again.''

Just seconds before, she'd have sworn nothing would persuade her to go along with such a notion. But the warmth in his tone of voice, the sympathy she saw in his eyes, had her suddenly thinking, *Why not?*

It had been months since she'd known any real excitement; longer still since she'd met a man as attractive as he was. And it wasn't as if they'd be alone. Fran and Adam would be there, and so would her parents, along with just about everyone else in town. If it turned out that she and Michael D'Alessandro had nothing to say to each other after the first half hour, there'd be plenty of other people willing to carry the conversational ball for the rest of the evening.

"Perhaps it is," she agreed. "All right. If you're still here and of the same mind next week at this time, I'll be glad of your company."

He subjected her to another of those long, intense looks. "You can count on it, Camille," he said. "I'm not going anywhere, any time soon."

She hadn't expected to see him again before the night of the gala, but avoiding anyone in a town as small as Calder was near to impossible, especially when that person was as eye-catching as Michael D'Alessandro. Over the next three days, she ran into him on three different occasions.

The first time they met was at Dolly's Coffee House. Camille and Jeremy were sitting at one of the outside tables, he with an ice cream cone and she with an iced cappuccino, when her Saturday night escort suddenly showed up. He stopped just long enough to say hello, let his glance linger a moment on Jeremy, and observe, "He's a fine-looking boy, Camille. You must be very proud."

"I am," she said. "And very lucky, too." Then, fearing her reply sounded unnecessarily clipped, felt obliged to add, "Would you care to join us?"

"Wish I could," he said with what seemed to be sincere regret, "but I'm meeting Adam Knowlton and a couple of his associates in a few minutes."

Later that morning, they ran into him again in the delicatessen. "Thought I'd put together a picnic lunch and eat down by the river," he said. "I'm told there's a swimming hole just outside town that's well worth a visit on a day like this." Then, seeing the way Jeremy's face lit up, added, "Don't suppose I can talk *you* into joining *me* this time?"

"Afraid not," she said. "We're due at the dentist in an hour for our six-month checkups."

Then, early on Tuesday afternoon, he drove into the service station on the highway right after she did, and pulled up to the gas pump behind hers.

"I'm on my way into San Francisco," he told her, coming to her car and bending almost double to look in the window while the attendant checked under the hood. "Thought I'd better fuel up here, rather than risk running short in the tunnel or on the Bay Bridge."

If it hadn't been preposterous, she'd have thought he was deliberately seeking her out, but after this opening comment, he seemed more interested in Jeremy than her, joking about his being the back-seat navigator for mom and a lot of other nonsense.

Again, Jeremy flowered under the attention. Apropos of nothing, he announced, "I've got teeth!" and bared them in all their pearly infant glory.

Michael D'Alessandro had teeth, too, and promptly showed them off in a smile that, annoyingly, set Camille's heart to fluttering. "You sure have, pal," he said. "Bet your dentist gave you a gold star for looking after them so well." He swung his glance back to her with obvious reluctance. "I guess I should get going."

"Yes. Do you have friends in the city?"

As it had the day they'd met, a brief cloud of sorrow dimmed his smile. "I...wouldn't say that, exactly. Just getting to know the area better, that's all."

She'd asked purely to be polite, and wondered why such a straightforward question made him uncomfortable. From the little she'd seen, he didn't strike her as a man easily put offstride.

Seeming to recognize that his hesitancy was out of character, he said, "I found Golden Gate Park the other day and thought I'd explore it further. It's huge."

She nodded. "Over a thousand acres, I believe. Just don't get caught in the rush hour traffic on the way back to Calder. It's a dreadful commute."

"So I've discovered. I plan to stay downtown well into the evening."

The attendant slammed down her car hood, wiped his hands on a rag, and gave her the thumbs-up sign. "Everything looks good, Ms. Whitfield."

"Well…!" She offered Michael D'Alessandro a cool smile. "See you on Saturday, if not before."

"It'll be before," he told her. "The Knowltons invited me to dinner the day after tomorrow, and I understand you'll be there, as well."

"Really?" It was her turn to be caught offguard. "We usually do get together on Thursdays but I hadn't realized Fran had asked you to join us."

"I think she feels sorry for me wandering around on my own, so she's taken me under her wing."

Camille thought Fran's motives were more devious than that, but she wasn't about to put ideas in his head by saying so.

Fran poured the last of the Chardonnay into their glasses, dropped into the chair next to Camille's, and kicked off her shoes. "Well, was the evening as bad as you thought it'd be?"

"Bad?" Camille sipped her wine thoughtfully. "I

wouldn't say 'bad' so much as 'pointless.' Why go to all this trouble to cultivate an acquaintance with a man who's only passing through town? It might be different if he were moving here permanently.''

"Because he's a nice man, and it looks as if he and Adam are going to be doing business together, and it's my wifely duty to entertain a client."

"But why include me?"

Fran, who tended to favor forthrightness over tact, took an unusually long time to answer. Finally she said, "When was the last time you felt any kind of excitement about life?"

"I don't need excitement. I had enough of that trying to keep my marriage intact. These days, I'm happy to settle for peaceful and uneventful."

"You're too young and beautiful to settle for anything, least of all that."

"I'm thirty years old, Fran."

"Exactly! And most of the time, you talk and act as if you're pushing ninety!" Fran leaned forward emphatically. "But you came alive tonight, Camille. The old sparkle was back in your eye. And we both know why."

"If you're suggesting Michael D'Alessandro's the reason—"

"He's the reason, all right! He flirted with you—in an entirely gentlemanly way, I might add—and you flirted right back. He made you laugh, and he made you blush almost as much as you're blushing now."

"For heaven's sake, I did not *flirt!*"

"You didn't hoist up your skirt and fling yourself in his lap, perhaps, but I saw you giving him the old eyeball treatment."

"He was my bridge partner. I was trying to warn him not to overbid."

Openly snickering, Fran said, "I see. And I suppose when you were ogling him during dinner, you were trying to warn him there might be caterpillars in his salad?"

Camille slammed down her wineglass with rather more force than was good for it. "I'm not up for this discussion tonight. I'm going home."

"Just because I'm pointing out truths you'd prefer not to hear is no reason to take it out on my good Steuben crystal," Fran said equably. "Nor do I understand why you're getting so hot about this. There's absolutely nothing wrong with your finding a man attractive. Nowhere is it written that a divorced woman has to shut herself off from the opposite sex and act as if she's taken holy orders."

"But I don't know this particular man! How often do I have to repeat that before it sinks in with you, Fran?"

"Most adult relationships start out that way, my dear. It's what comes of *getting to know* someone that counts."

"Michael D'Alessandro isn't going to be around long enough for me to get to know him—at least, not in any meaningful fashion."

"So forget 'meaningful' and just have a fling. Heaven knows, you're ripe for one, and the opportunity's staring you in the face. Lighten up and have some fun for a change. You might find you like it."

Was it possible Fran was right, and she *was* ripe for a fling? Did that explain the heady feeling that had begun during dinner and lasted throughout the short drive from the Knowltons' house to her own—as if she were a little giddy from too much champagne, even though she'd had only two and half glasses of wine all night? And if so, might she not be better off experimenting with a man who just happened to be passing through, rather than someone she'd known all her life? At least that way, if the whole thing turned out to be a disaster, he wouldn't always be around to remind her of it.

The idea percolated at the back of Camille's mind all the time she was arming her home security system for the night, sending Nori, her Japanese nanny, off to bed, and making a last check on Jeremy. By the time she, too, was ready to turn in, she'd half convinced herself Fran was right, and the prospect of being escorted to the gala by Michael D'Alessandro didn't seem such a bad idea, after all. In fact, it had assumed intriguing new possibilities.

Kay's condition seemed to have deteriorated by the Friday. After leaving her, Michael drove along the western rim of Golden Gate Park, found his usual bench overlooking the water, and sat there, elbows on his knees, fingers steepled in front of his mouth.

A light mist had drifted in earlier, turning the June evening cool and leaving that particular stretch of park almost deserted. Just as well. If he was going to start bawling, he didn't need an audience.

"How much longer?" he'd asked the nurse, before he left the hospital.

She'd shaken her head. "Maybe weeks, maybe days. It's hard to tell."

He'd asked his next question before and already knew the answer. Chemotherapy had failed, radiation had failed. Still, he'd had to ask again, "Is there nothing that can be done for her?"

"We're keeping her comfortable, Mr. D'Alessandro. I'm afraid that's the most we can offer. If she'd seen a doctor and been diagnosed sooner...."

His sense of helplessness had spilled over into anger. "Why the devil didn't she? She had medical insurance."

The nurse shrugged sympathetically. "Perhaps she was

afraid of what she'd find out. A lot of people are. By the time she did come for help, it was too late.''

Too late in more ways than one!

Just before he left her, Kay had pinned him in a haunted, pleading gaze. ''I'd like to see my baby, Mike...just once...just for a minute. Couldn't you find a way... please...?''

But she didn't know how she looked now; had no idea how terrifying a three-and-a-half-year old would find her. Once again, she'd left it too late. And even if she hadn't, there was no way he could have arranged a visit without telling Camille the whole story—which opened up another can of worms he wished didn't exist.

As a woman, Camille Whitfield was off limits to him. He knew that with utter certainty and to behave as he had last night would bring nothing but disaster. Yet she pulled him like a magnet.

He tried to justify his response by telling himself he had to cozy up to her if he wanted to get closer to his son. The woman was no longer married, after all, nor, as far as he could determine, involved with another man, so what was wrong with cultivating a bit of a relationship? He'd even gone the route of thinking that the reason he found her so attractive lay in the fact that, physically, she was the antithesis of Kay: clear-eyed, sweetly fleshed, golden.

There was no doubt that seeing his ex-wife in her present condition affected him more deeply than he'd ever expected. Each time he left her in that narrow, sterile hospital room, every instinct cried out for him to hold on to a warm, healthy body and let it drive away the specter of the woman he used to know.

Maybe that was natural enough. But if so, it shouldn't be Camille Whitfield's body he reached for! Bad enough he was already using her. To compound the sin by encouraging anything that might fan the flames of sexual attraction between them was out of the question and he simply couldn't allow it to happen.

It couldn't be Jeremy he held on to either, even though he'd have given ten years of his life to be able to wrap his arms around that little boy and hug him close to his heart. The same blood might run in their veins, but circumstance had relegated him to the role of friendly stranger in his son's life. He couldn't do anything which might jeopardize strengthening so fragile a link.

Hell, what a mess!

Lifting his head, he stared out at the blurred lights pricking the darkness—and knew it wasn't mist obscuring his vision, it was tears. How many times had he come to this spot to get himself back together after visiting Kay? How often had he wound up sniveling like a kid? And how many more times, before it was over for her?

Damn! He hadn't been a tenth as broken up when their marriage went bad. Been glad to see the back of her, in fact. So why all this emotion now when it was too late to do either of them any good?

Swiping an impatient hand over his eyes, he hauled himself off the bench and started back to where he'd left the car. Enough of the brooding and self-pity. He'd promised Kay he'd find a way to photograph the child and bring her a copy.

Sitting there asking questions no one could answer wasn't going to get the job done. He'd be better off thinking up ways to wheedle his way further into Camille Whitfield's good graces without compromising his integrity any more than he already had—and hope to high heaven he wouldn't give in to temptation along the way.

CHAPTER TWO

THANKFULLY, the madness passed and she was able to withstand Fran's suggestion that being seen on the arm of a "hunk" warranted buying a new dress for the gala. When Saturday came, Camille didn't even haul out the family diamonds, even though she knew her mother would comment on their non-appearance.

Instead she picked out a black chiffon creation she'd worn several times before, and teamed it with black silk pumps and the black pearl choker and earrings her father had brought back for her from one of his overseas business trips.

"Good grief, who died?" Fran exclaimed, when she and Camille met for pre-dinner drinks on the terrace of the country club that night. "Don't tell me you offed your date?"

"No," Camille said sweetly. "If I were bent on murder, old friend, you'd be my choice of victim. Michael's in the lobby, buying raffle tickets."

"Well, at least he's graduated to being called 'Michael' instead of 'that man' or worse! Is he in funereal garb as well?"

"He's wearing a very nice dinner suit."

"And looks delicious in it, I'm sure."

Camille pressed her lips together, but the smile crept through anyway. "As a matter of fact, he does. And unlike you, he sees nothing wrong with *my* outfit, either."

Actually, what he'd said when he came to pick her up at the house was, "Holy cow!" but the way his eyes had swept her from head to toe told her he very much liked what he saw.

"Well, that's what matters." Fran tipped her head to one side and inspected Camille again. "And on second thought, maybe there is something to be said for the contradictory way you've done yourself up—all that demure black giving out a touch-me-not message, while the neckline begs 'Take a peek!' It's enough to drive any red-blooded man off the rails."

"What?"

"You heard!" Fran glanced over her shoulder to the doors leading into the clubhouse. "Please close your mouth and stop hyperventilating, Camille. Your escort and my husband are about to descend on us bearing gifts, and you're wasting all the trouble you've gone to to look alluring by gaping like a landed fish." Then, without missing a beat, she sang out blithely, "Hello, Michael! So nice to see you again. I was just admiring Camille's dress. Lovely, isn't it?"

"Very nice indeed."

An acceptable enough response, Camille supposed, but definitely lacking his earlier moment of spontaneous approval. In fact, when she came to think about it, apart from that initial burst of enthusiasm, his manner toward her had tended to be as formal as his attire.

He handed her a glass of champagne without quite touching her fingers, then stood a respectable distance away and showed no inclination at all to look down the front of her dress, or at any other part of her, come to that! For all the interest he showed, she might as well have been just another potted plant. What confounded her the most, though, was that she felt so let down about it!

He showed no such reticence with the Knowltons, laughing and chatting with them as comfortably as if they'd all grown up playing in the same sandbox, so she was glad when her mother and father eventually showed up. At least she could count on *them* not to ignore her.

"Come and meet Michael D'Alessandro, Camille's date for the evening," Fran caroled, after the obligatory round of air kisses and greetings. "Michael, this is Glenda and David Younge, Camille's parents."

"D'Alessandro? I'm not familiar with the name," her mother said, offering the tips of her fingers in a handshake. "You're not from around here, are you, Mr. D'Alessandro?"

"No, ma'am," he replied. "I'm Canadian."

"Visiting, are you?" Glenda eyed him up and down, her faintly raised brows denoting some serious doubts about a man who, dinner suit and flawless manners notwithstanding, could have used a haircut and had calluses on his hands.

Her father's tactics were even worse. He inspected Michael over the top of his rimless glasses, and made no bones about quizzing him. "What do you do, young man?"

"I'm a building contractor, Mr. Younge."

"Commercial or industrial?"

"Residential."

"Humph! High end?"

"Very." He didn't try to hide his amusement.

"Any partners?"

"None."

"Except the bank, I imagine."

"Not even the bank, although I did have to call on them during a pretty thin period a few years back. But I'm out of the red now."

Her father digested that for a moment. "Must be a very small operation."

"I prefer to call it exclusive. My houses are custom de-signed, and I use only the best materials and trades."

"What makes you so sure that's what you're getting?"

"I know quality when I see it and I pay top dollar to acquire it. There's nothing shabby about the way I do busi-ness."

"I admire your confidence," her father said, but his tone suggested "arrogance" might better fit the description. He wasn't used to having a man thirty years his junior speak to him as if they were equals.

But Michael didn't seem at all put out at being cross-examined, Camille thought resentfully, so why did he con-tinue giving her the cold shoulder all through dinner and make no effort to engage her in a private tête-à-tête—no effort to *flirt* with her, as he had on the Thursday evening?

It wasn't until the live music started and everyone else at their table was on the dance floor that, left with little option other than deserting her altogether, he said, "Well, Camille, are you happy with the evening's turnout?"

"Yes. Raising funds for the shelter is a project very dear to my heart, and I think we'll make a lot of money tonight. I couldn't be more pleased."

His sudden smile washed over her like warm honey. "Should I take that to mean you're not finding it too em-barrassing having me as your escort, after all?"

"I'd be enjoying it more if you asked me to dance," she said boldly. "You've been so distant, I'm beginning to think you're the one who's embarrassed."

"Then either I'm sending out the wrong message, or you're not reading me correctly." He pushed back his chair, and offered her his hand. "On your feet, madam. Let's go show 'em how it's done."

Given that she'd practically forced him into dancing with her, she half expected he'd be more the one-two-three-four box step sort of partner than one who'd lead a woman through a foxtrot without missing a beat, *and* manage to hold a conversation at the same time—which just went to show it wasn't wise to make assumptions about people one barely knew.

"So tell me," he began, weaving a deft path between the couples packed on the floor, "how long have you been sponsoring this women's shelter?"

"Almost four years. This is our third fund-raising gala."

He executed a sweeping turn and cut a swath through the crowd. "And what prompted you to take on such a project in the first place?"

"My son's birth mother," she said, then let out a tiny yelp as his shoe ground down on her foot.

"Sorry," he muttered, placing his hand more firmly in the small of her back. "It was step on you or the fat lady behind you, and she's bigger than I am! Your son's...*birth mother,* you say?"

"Jeremy's adopted," she told him. "I'd forgotten you wouldn't know that. We brought him home right before Christmas, when he was just five days old."

"Did you indeed."

"Yes." She smiled, that memory, at least, untarnished by what came after. Within months of Jeremy's birth, Todd had started drinking again and dabbling in drugs. She'd dreaded the unpredictability that came with his addiction: the rages, followed by undignified displays of remorse; the abandonment of personal and professional responsibility. "Jeremy was the best Christmas gift I ever received."

"I'm sure he was," Michael said, rather grimly she thought, "but I don't see the connection between that and your deciding to finance a women's shelter."

"If you'd known his birth mother, you would. She was in such dire straits, poor thing."

"At having to give up her child?"

"To some extent, yes. But mostly at having no other choice."

"I'm not sure I follow you. No one held a gun to her head, surely?"

"Not literally, perhaps, but he might as well have."

"He?"

"Her husband."

"You make him sound like a monster."

"He was." Her dance partner didn't know his own strength. She winced at the sudden crushing grip of his hand around hers as he swung her into another reverse turn. "He abandoned her with no means of support. If we hadn't met her when we did, I hate to think what might have become of her and her baby."

Michael made a sort of choking noise and she looked up to find him staring at her with eyes blazing such an electric shade of blue that they put to shame the spotlights reflecting off the twirling crystal ball overhead.

"I know," she said, giving the satin lapel of his dinner jacket a consoling pat. "It's hard to believe a man could be so wickedly unfeeling."

"Isn't it, though!"

"On the other hand, if he hadn't behaved so badly, I wouldn't be a mother today."

Michael stretched his neck, as if his shirt collar were a size too small. "Did it ever occur to you there might be another side to this story—one which doesn't paint the guy in quite such a bad light?"

"When a pregnant woman's practically living on the street, Michael, there *is* no other side to the story!"

The music ended just then which was a good thing because he seemed to be on the verge of an asthma attack, or something. Looking rather flushed, he walked her back to their table but when her mother suggested he take her in a turn around the floor, he abruptly refused. "I need some fresh air," he said. "Excuse me, please."

"He doesn't look very well," Fran said, staring after him as he fairly bolted for the door. "I hope he's all right."

"Might be something he ate," Camille's father said. "I thought the shrimp seemed a bit off."

Mightily offended at being rejected by someone she'd ordinarily have dismissed as being unworthy of notice, her mother was not nearly so disposed to be charitable. "Or else his rented suit's a shade too tight. I don't think it was designed to accommodate a man of his proportions."

"What's that supposed to mean, Mother?" Although puzzled herself by his behavior, Camille felt obligated to spring to his defense.

Glenda Younge gave a dismissive shrug. "The man's got the build of a laborer. He belongs in dungarees."

"If I'd known you'd take such exception to his appearance, I'd have arranged for us to sit at another table."

"Why, dear!" Her mother reared back, one hand splayed across the emeralds at her throat. "I had no idea you felt so strongly about him!"

Until that moment, nor had Camille. Feeling the need to champion a man manifestly able to look after himself surprised her as much as it did her mother. "It isn't him personally," she said. "I'd feel the same about any guest of mine being subjected to insult, especially by a member of my family."

"I made sure he was well out of earshot before I spoke my mind and I hardly think anyone else here will feel the need to repeat what I said." Glenda, never one to concede an argument if she could possibly avoid it, attacked from another angle. "As for his being your guest, Camille, I was of the impression he'd bought his own way in here. He made a big enough point about contributing to a worthy cause.''

"Let it rest, Glenda,'' her husband warned. "He's a bit too full of himself, I admit, but there's nothing wrong with a man working for a living.''

"Oh, David, please don't you start defending him, too! We all know he's not *one of us*. What's so terrible about stating out the obvious?''

"I'm not sure I know what being *one of us* really amounts to,'' Fran put in, "but for what my opinion's worth, I happen to like Michael.''

Again, Camille surprised herself. "So do I. Very much. And while you might find him not quite upper-class enough for your refined tastes, Mother, I'm willing to bet he'd never make a public fool of himself the way Todd did the first time we held this gala. I doubt my father and Adam are going to have to pick him up, dead drunk, off the floor and carry him to the car before the evening's half over.''

Her mother let out a forbearing sigh. "Camille, this isn't about Todd's appalling behavior, it's about your sudden fascination for—''

"You're right, Mother, it isn't about Todd. It's about a man who's done nothing to deserve your contempt, so if you'll all excuse me, I'm going to go after him and make sure he knows he's welcome to join us again when he feels up to it.''

She found him down near the man-made lake below the terrace, staring at the sweep of the fairway. He stood so unnervingly still, it was as if the essence of the man had flown away to some other place and left behind just the shell of his body.

Tentatively, she touched his arm. "Michael? Is something wrong?''

"Yes."

She waited for him to elaborate, and when it became obvious he wasn't going to, said, "Can you tell me about it?"

When at last he turned to her, his eyes were so empty she might have been looking at a dead man. She had no idea whether he was angry, or ill, or just very tired. She did know the way he was acting frightened her. "No. You're the last person I can talk to," he said.

"Why?"

He inhaled so deeply, the starch in his shirt crackled. "I have no business being here with you tonight—no right at all cultivating an acquaintance with you."

"Because we come from different worlds?"

He let out a bark of laughter. "More than you can begin to imagine!"

"If you're talking about money—"

"I wasn't, but since you mentioned it, we're hardly in the same tax bracket. I bet the closest you've ever come to a man like me before is the last time you had to call in a plumber. Small wonder your mother just about swallowed her emeralds when she laid eyes on me. She probably thinks you've lost your mind."

"What if I don't care what my mother thinks?" She slid her fingers down the sleeve of his jacket and found his hand. "I took charge of my life a long time ago, Michael. I choose who I want to spend time with, and tonight I want to be with you."

"And exactly who do you think I am, Camille?"

"The man who, two days ago, made eyes at me across the Knowltons' dinner table. The same man whose smile reminded me I'm more than a mother, I'm a woman, too."

"Don't go down that road, Camille! It's a dead end."

He tried to withdraw his hand, but she wouldn't let him.

She caught it in both of hers and turning it over, traced her fingertips over the calluses on his palm. "Why? What's changed since Thursday, Michael? If it's something about me—something I said or did—please give me the chance to put things right again."

"It isn't you," he muttered. "You're…lovely."

"But no longer desirable?" She moved closer. Enough to detect the faint scent of soap on his skin. Enough that the warmth of his body feathered over her bare arms and reached inside the low neckline of her dress. "Is that what you're really saying, Michael?"

A tremor ran through him. "No."

"Then why are you keeping me at such a distance?"

"Because we're not a couple of high school kids looking for any chance we can find to grope each other!"

"But we *are* consenting adults," she said, trying to smother the pleading tone creeping into her voice. "And rolling around in the bushes is a far cry from treating someone as if you're afraid, if you get too close, they might infect you with the plague."

"Sorry if you feel I've short-changed you," he sneered. "Maybe this'll make you feel better."

He yanked her against him and bent to pin her mouth beneath his, his manner so far removed from tender that she might as well have been kissed by a brick wall. At least, that's the way things started out. But no sooner had their lips made contact than the spark he'd tried to deny ignited as brilliantly as a burst of fireworks across the night sky.

If it scorched her, it seemed almost to destroy him. A groan escaped him, torn reluctantly from some deep well of pain inside. The unyielding pressure of his mouth softened to a caress. His hands let go their iron grip of her waist and smoothed a hypnotic path up her spine. She felt his fingers steal through her hair, the brush of his eyelashes against her brow, the heavy, uneven beat of his heart against her breast.

She was scarcely a novice where lovemaking was concerned. For at least seven of the eight years she and Todd had been married, they'd tried every means known to man and science to conceive a child. Ovulation charts, fertility thermometers, candlelight, body oils, seductive music, chocolate, oysters, massages—*atmosphere* by the bushel, not to mention plain old-fashioned intercourse, they'd tried them all.

But not once in all those times had she experienced the wild blossoming of pleasure she found in Michael D'Alessandro's arms—as if she'd faint if he didn't stop. As if she'd die if he did.

She wound her arms around his neck and clung to him. Scarcely waited for the questing nudge of his lips against hers before she opened to admit him. As to what followed…how was it possible that his probing exploration of her mouth could effect such far-reaching results? How could the pulsing rhythm of his tongue engaging hers find an echoing spasm between her legs—as if a direct line of contact were hot-wired between the two zones? When had her pelvis taken it upon itself to undulate against his and revel in the painful pressure of his arousal?

Sweet heaven, where were her scruples that when he began inching her dress up past her knees, she parted her thighs in wanton surrender?

He must have asked himself the same question and not liked the answer. "Cripes!" he exclaimed, wrenching his mouth away from hers and releasing her so suddenly she almost fell over. "You really are willing to roll around in the bushes, aren't you?"

If half the town had caught her having sex stark naked

in the middle of Calder's main street, she couldn't have been more humiliated. Face burning, hand scrubbing at her mouth, feet stumbling over themselves, she struggled to recoup her dignity. To fell him with a few well-chosen words so pithy he'd be left speechless.

Instead, she heard disgust in his voice, saw it in his expression, and was struck dumb herself. Because he was right: she *would* have rolled in the bushes with him, if he'd allowed it. She'd have guided his hand inside her panties and let him touch her until she was ready to scream for him to fill her with his big, vibrant masculine strength.

She must be mad!

He buttoned his dinner jacket, and shot his shirt cuffs into place. "If you don't want people asking awkward questions, you'd better pay a visit to the powder room before you go back to your table. You look a bit disheveled."

"If anyone asks questions," she shot back, "I'll refer them to you."

"Not a chance! I've had all the country club hoo-ha I can take for one night. I'm out of here, sweetheart. I'd offer to drive you home, but under the circumstances—"

"Oh, please! Don't do me any more favors!"

He shrugged and, without another word, loped up the steps to the terrace. By the time she found her way there, he'd already disappeared around the side of the clubhouse. And a good thing, too. If he'd hung around another moment, he'd have seen she was crying and that was one satisfaction she wouldn't afford him.

Face averted, she scuttled through the foyer to the ladies' room and locked herself in the nearest stall. The evening, which had started out so full of promise, had ended in a shambles. This was one fund-raising gala she couldn't wait to forget.

*   *   *

Of course, he was an utter jerk. But she had to share some of the blame, coming on to him like that and practically begging him to do her! Sheesh, what did she think? That he was dead from the waist down? That he was as blind as he must be stupid, not to have noticed she outshone every woman in the room when it came to sheer sex appeal?

But trying to excuse his behavior as he hurled the car around the narrow curves of the road back to Calder did nothing to erase the image of her wide-eyed hurt, and even less to diminish the lingering ache of desire which had damn near crippled him.

His B and B lay on the far side of town, right on the river. He parked on the graveled area reserved for guest cars, but instead of letting himself into the house, followed a path running under a flower-draped trellis to the water. No point in trying to sleep. He needed to get her out of his system first. Wash away the taste of her with a blast of night air. Rid himself of the scent of her. Forget the texture of her skin, her hair, her mouth.

"If I hadn't been around to take that phone call a couple of weeks back, I wouldn't be in this mess now," he complained to the night at large.

The river rolled on by, scarcely breaking a ripple. *Too late, buddy!*

True enough. It had been too late the minute the woman on the other end of the line had opened her mouth.

"My name's Diana Moon," she'd said. "I'm a volunteer at St. Mary's Hospital in San Francisco and I'm calling on behalf of Rita Osborne, a patient in our oncology unit."

It had taken him a minute to clue in because although Kay had been born Rita Kay Osborne, she'd always gone by her middle name, and had taken D'Alessandro as her surname after their marriage. By the time he'd made the connection, the ominous connotation behind *oncology unit* had sunk home, and the die was cast. Divorced or not, he couldn't turn his back on her, knowing she was dying. Probably couldn't have, even if she'd been a stranger. To learn she was asking for him merely added extra poignancy to the whole sorry business.

He'd left Doug Russell, his chief foreman, in charge, and flown down to San Francisco the next day, braced to cope with the physical devastation of Kay's illness and willing to do whatever he could to help ease her final days. But the sight of her poor ravaged body—emaciated, bloodless, her once glorious auburn hair reduced to a few pale wisps, her milky skin turned bilious yellow—did not hit home quite as hard as the bombshell she handed him when he arrived at her bedside.

We had a baby, Mike...a son. I gave him away....

That he hadn't been able to think straight since was his only excuse for the way he'd acted tonight. Because if he'd stopped to use his brains, he'd have realized that alienating Camille accomplished nothing. She was his passport to Jeremy. He needed her in ways she couldn't begin to imagine.

Stooping, he sent a rock skipping over the moonlit surface of the water and watched the ripples spread toward the far bank in a complex, glimmering chain. Sort of like his life, right now, he mused.

Two weeks ago, he'd been single, unattached, and successful. The lean years were behind him, the money rolling in, his life, like his financial records, an open book in perfect order.

Today he was an undercover father lusting after a woman he couldn't have; a liar, a sneak, and now, as the final icing on the cake, supposedly an abusive ex-husband.

He could hardly wait to find out what tomorrow would bring!

CHAPTER THREE

IF SHE'D known who it was ringing her bell at eleven o'clock the next morning, she'd have slipped into something less revealing before answering. Better yet, she wouldn't have answered at all. But expecting it was Fran, whom she knew must be eaten up with curiosity about what had gone awry the night before, Camille left Jeremy splashing in the pool under Nori's watchful eye and flung open the front door without a second thought.

Fran, though, didn't top six feet by at least three inches, or sport the kind of shoulders associated with beefcake movie stars in their prime. She didn't wear khaki shorts that showed off a pair of tanned athletic legs dusted with fine black hair. And she did not, as a rule, look as if she were about to have a seizure at the sight of Camille in a bathing suit.

"I know," Michael D'Alessandro began, eyeing all the skin she was showing with undisguised interest and not the least bit deterred by what she hoped was the icy glare she offered him in return. "I'm probably the last person you want to see."

"That's putting it mildly."

"I'm a jackass."

"Yes."

"Your mother would probably like to see me strung up by the thumbs."

"Leave my mother out of this," she shot back. "It's what *I*'d like to see happen that you need to worry about."

"I wish I could explain."

Explain reducing her to molten lava with his expert seduction, then tossing her aside and leaving her to return to the gala alone to face her family and friends? "Don't even try. There's no excusing the way you behaved. I've never been so embarrassed in my life."

"I kinda figured that might be the case."

"Then it should come as no surprise that you're not welcome in my house. I'm giving you exactly thirty seconds to vacate the premises."

"At least let me apologize before you turn the rotweilers loose on me."

The man had the audacity to smile as he said that and she, dolt that she was, had a hard time not smiling back. "I don't keep rotweilers. Until I met you, there was never any need."

"Until *I* met *you*," he said, his voice as smooth as warm satin against her skin, "I never behaved like a maniac on the loose. But then, I've never met a woman like you before, either, so I'm a bit at sea on the proper protocol."

Oh, the nerve of the man, trying to look angelic and remorseful all the time his insolent gaze roamed over her without a shred of shame! "It's no great mystery," she said tartly. "In the kind of social situation we shared last night, it's customary for a gentleman to treat his dinner partner with the same courtesy and respect that she extends to him."

"I know." He tried to look suitably humble, but the devil lurking in his eyes was laughing. "However, when the lady in question persists in turning the social situation into a romantic tryst beneath the stars, a gentleman's better instincts tend to get lost in more…earthy concerns."

"Are you suggesting that I deliberately set out to…to…well, to…?"

"Get me so hot I couldn't see straight?"

Shocked by such a blunt assessment, she backed away. "I had no such intention!"

"Didn't you?" he said, losing no time getting his foot in the door and stalking her across the foyer. "Wasn't that why you followed me outside?"

"Certainly not!" She had never sounded more definite in her life. Neither had she ever blushed so furiously that even her ankles turned pink!

"Mmm-hmm." He gave her a pitying smile, the kind which said, *Come off it, Camille! I wasn't born yesterday and neither were you!*

"I thought you weren't feeling well and came after you to see if there was anything I could do."

"You came after me because you thought I no longer found you attractive and you wanted to know why."

She opened her mouth to deny it, but giving voice to such a barefaced lie put a stranglehold on her vocal cords and rendered her mute. Was there to be no end to her humiliation?

He touched his forefinger to the underside of her lower lip and pushed it back where it belonged. "In case I left you in any doubt, I find you damn near irresistible, Camille."

He sounded as if he really meant it; as if, in having hurt her, he'd hurt himself. It had been so long since a man had spoken to her like that, with his voice cloaked in tender regret—as if she mattered, as if he *cared!*—that her eyes filled and her chin quivered.

Noticing, he hooked his finger in the strap of her bathing suit and tugged her toward him. "If you thought my behavior was out of line last night," he said, his mouth inching dangerously close to hers, "you should know that I'm fighting a serious urge to kiss you again now, and if you start crying, I don't hold out any guarantee that I'll be able to control myself.''

"I'm not sure that I want you to,'' she whimpered.

"Oh, brother!'' He closed his eyes and exhaled, his breath ruffling sweetly over her face. "I'm in trouble!''

"Not necessarily.''

The back of his finger slid from her shoulder to graze the upper slope of her breast. "Are you sure you know what you're saying? I'm not made of stone, Camille, and you're not exactly dressed to receive company. Do you really want to run the risk of Jeremy walking in on us?''

"Heavens, no!'' She pulled away and slapped her crossed arms over her breasts before he noticed how animated they'd become at the prospect of a little morning seduction. "Thank goodness one of us has some sense!''

He shot her a cajoling glance. "Does that mean I'm forgiven for last night?''

She'd never been much good at holding a grudge. An optimist herself, she looked for the best in other people; wanted to believe that their motives were pure, their intentions good. And the more she saw of Michael D'Alessandro, the more she sensed that his was a strength drawn as much on integrity as physical power.

"I think we should forgive each other and move on,'' she said, stepping well out of the reach of temptation before she weakened and begged him to throw caution to the winds and follow his instincts. She'd wound up in enough trouble last night when she was fully clothed. Playing fast and loose with fire when she had barely a stitch on was asking to be burned.

"In that case, I have something in my car I'd like to give to Jeremy—with your permission, of course. Come and tell me what you think.''

Slinging an arm around her shoulders, he steered her

outside to his car and lifted the hatchback. "What do you think of that?" he said, nodding at the fire-engine-red car inside.

She recognized it at once. It had been donated by a local businessman with a passion for vintage cars, and was a scaled-down working reproduction of a 1920 roadster, perfect to every last detail. "I know it's one of the items raffled off last night and that half the fathers in this town hoped they'd be taking it home with them. How did you come by it?"

"Someone phoned me at the B and B this morning to tell me I'd won it." He stroked an admiring hand over the gleaming chrome rear fender. "It's a beauty, and I hoped, since I've missed out on so many—" He stopped suddenly, his expression startled, as if he'd caught himself about to say something untoward. It took him a moment before he recovered enough to continue, "Well, I hoped you'd let me give it to Jeremy."

"Michael!" she protested. "I'm the one who solicited donations for the raffle. I know what that toy's worth and I can't possibly let you give it to a child you barely know."

"Why not? There's no one else I'd sooner see have it, and as for how much it cost...." He shrugged. "I got it for the price of a couple of tickets. A pretty cheap way to give a boy pleasure, wouldn't you say?"

"But isn't there someone at home you'd rather save it for?"

"I don't have children waiting there for me, if that's what you're asking."

Well, she *had* wondered about that, given that he'd mentioned he'd been married at one time, but she hadn't expected touching on the subject would trigger quite such a vehement reaction in him.

As if realizing he'd been abrupt, he said lightly, "My

cousin Dante and his wife have four-year-old twins, but those boys already have enough toys to fill a barn. They don't need any more.'' He gestured at the roadster. ''In any case, I'll be flying home, and there's no way this is going to fit in my carry-on bag.''

''Jeremy isn't exactly lacking when it comes to play-things either, you know.''

''I'm not suggesting he is.''

''I know. I just feel I'm taking advantage of your gen-erosity. Wouldn't you rather give the car to charity—maybe to a children's hospice, or even to our shelter? Many of the women we help are mothers with small children and a toy like this—''

''Jeremy will have a blast with it and I'd like to see it go to him.'' His tone was edging toward sharp again, and he made a conscious effort to moderate it. ''Look, I'll make a deal with you. Let him have it for now, and when he outgrows it in a year or two, you have my permission to donate it wherever you think it will do the most good.''

My, the man was stubborn! But he was also right. Jeremy *would* be in seventh heaven. ''Well…okay! You've con-vinced me. I'll go get him out of the pool and into some dry clothes.''

His face broke into the smile she couldn't resist. Was there a woman alive who could? ''Terrific! While you're doing that, I'll unload the car.''

The mixture of awe and delight reflected on Jeremy's face when he saw his gift left Camille midway between laughter and tears. It was impossible not to enjoy his plea-sure—and equally impossible not to be aware yet again of how much he missed not having a father around to share such moments with him.

After his initial shriek of delight and wide-eyed, ''Wow, Mommy, look!'' she was relegated to the role of spectator as he and Michael got down to the serious man-to-man business of examining the car and figuring out how it worked.

"The thing is, buddy," Michael said, hunkering down beside him and flipping open the trunk, "your engine runs on these batteries in here."

"Cool!"

"Yeah, but it won't be so cool if they get drained. So when you're finished playing for the day, you have to take them out like this, see?"

"But not 'til I park, right?"

Michael buried a grin. "Right. When you've parked, they need to be plugged into an electrical outlet to recharge so that you're ready to roll again the next day. Think you can sweet-talk your mom into doing that for you?"

"I can do it myself." Jeremy puffed out his chest with pride. "I do it for my remote control truck. Mom showed me how."

"No kidding." Michael looked appropriately impressed. "I guess you're more grown up than I realized."

"I'm *three!*"

"That's pretty grown up, all right."

"Can I drive now?"

"Sure, as long as you remember to steer straight and brake when you want to slow down, otherwise you'll be plowing through your mom's flower beds and I'll be for the high jump." He held open the door while Jeremy climbed into the driver's seat, then stood back and gave him the thumbs-up. "Hit the road, Jack!"

Camille held her breath, all at once unsure she'd made the right decision. "How fast can that thing go, Michael?"

"About as fast as this," he assured her, his long-legged stride keeping easy pace as Jeremy took off around the circular turn-around at the foot of the steps. "Don't worry,

I'll stay with him until he's got the hang of things, and as long as you keep the driveway gates closed so he can't wander out into traffic, he'll be fine.''

He really was a nice man, she thought; patient, kind, and generous not just with material things, but with his time and the attention he paid to her little boy. ''I've got my camera in the car,'' he said to her, at one point. ''Do you mind if I take a couple of shots to record the moment, before the novelty wears off?''

''Of course not. I should have thought of it myself.''

He snapped a picture of Jeremy beaming behind the wheel, and another of him polishing the hood of the car with the tail of his T-shirt, then caught her offguard and took one of her, as well. Later, when Jeremy asked him to play football, Michael made a big production of trying to wrestle the ball away from him and not succeeding.

Jeremy was in seventh heaven and would happily have kept him hopping all afternoon if Nori hadn't come out to say that lunch was ready.

Michael seemed genuinely sorry to see him leave. ''He's a real gem, Camille.''

''I know. And you were wonderful with him.''

''Yeah, well, he's easy to…like.'' He stuffed his hands in the pockets of his shorts, seeming almost uncomfortable with the compliment. ''Thanks for hearing me out—and for letting me unload my winnings on him.''

He gave a little salute and turned away with no mention of seeing her again. The possibility that their association had come to an end, that he might leave Calder and head home without so much as a goodbye, all at once struck her as unthinkable. ''You don't have to go just yet if you don't want to,'' she called out, seconds before he climbed into his car. ''You could stay for lunch—unless you have other plans, that is?''

''No plans,'' he said, loping back and coming to a stop so close to her that she could see her reflection in the pupils of his eyes. ''At least, not until later this afternoon.''

''Then please say you'll stay. I know Jeremy would like it.''

''Just Jeremy?'' His mouth twitched with amusement.

She flushed. ''All right, I'd like it, too.''

''You just talked me into it.''

Her heart beat a little tattoo against her ribs. ''It won't be anything fancy.''

''It doesn't have to be,'' he said. ''Just seeing you blush like that could turn dry bread and water into a feast.''

Her idea of fancy didn't coincide with his. Although a member of two of Vancouver's most revered clubs, when he was on the job he usually brown-bagged it for lunch, which meant something simple like a sandwich and fruit. He'd hang out with his employees, using the time to listen to their beefs and iron out any problems. Or, if the weather was really lousy, he'd take the whole crew down to the nearest hamburger joint.

Sushi on a sun-dappled terrace might be considered a ''nothing fancy'' lunch in Camille's world, but it was a ''special occasion'' treat in his.

What really stunned him, though, was the way Jeremy dug right in, wielding chopsticks better than most kids his age used a fork. Tuna, abalone, eel, pickled ginger—the whole lot went down the little red lane with equal relish.

''Quite the cosmopolitan little gourmet you've got there,'' Mike remarked.

''He loves Japanese food, and I have Nori to thank for it.'' Camille exchanged smiles with the tiny woman hovering over Jeremy, then lowered her voice to add, ''She's been with me from the day we brought him home from the hospital. I don't know how I'd have managed without her, especially since the divorce. She's been a second mother to him—not that that makes up for his not having his father around, of course.''

His father's around, sweetheart. You're sitting right next to him!

Hard-pressed not to spit out the truth and have done with, Mike turned his attention to a plate of California rolls and selected one. But either he needed more practice with chopsticks, or he was too preoccupied with his private dilemmas because the roll took on a life of its own, flipped loose and splattered on the table.

Jeremy burst into the same infectious giggle which had captured Mike's heart the first time he laid eyes on the boy. "You made a mess, Michael. You've got *gohan* all over your shirt.''

''Gohan?''

"Rice," Camille said. "He's picked up quite a bit of Japanese from Nori. Do you care for more tea?''

"No, thanks. I should be going. I've taken up enough of your time.''

He might be mouthing words he didn't mean, but she wasn't when she replied, ''Oh, please! We've hardly had any chance to visit privately.''

"Quit tempting me! I might wear out my welcome.''

"Don't be silly. Jeremy goes down for a half-hour nap once he's finished eating, so unless you really do have to rush off, do stay a little longer.''

He knew he ought to refuse and get out of there. The more time he spent with her, the more he liked what he saw—and so far that day, he'd seen a lot! Before they sat down to eat, she'd put on a long print shirt over her swimsuit, but she was still showing plenty of leg. On the other hand, there was a lot he still didn't know about his boy's life, so why pass up a heaven-sent chance to fill in some of the gaps—particularly those relating to the absent "father"?

"We can take our tea by the pool. It's cooler down by the water," she said, apparently mistaking his silence for reluctance.

As if he needed bribing!

Not only was the pool Olympic size, with a bridge and a mini-waterfall at one end, and a children's wading area off to one side, there was at least an acre of lawns surrounded by massed flower beds beyond the brick-paved deck.

"How do you manage the upkeep on all this?" he asked, joining her on a long cushioned swing shaded by a striped canvas awning. "Do you have a gardener, or does your ex-husband help out?"

Dumb question, of course. Any fool could see the grounds were professionally maintained, but he had to start somewhere, and if she thought he was a dim bulb for asking, she was too polite to let it show. "I have gardeners come in twice a week. My ex-husband hasn't been near the property since our divorce."

Interesting! "Is that your choice, or his?"

"Both. We stay out of each other's way. Our breakup wasn't exactly amicable." She toed the swing into motion and looked at him over the rim of her teacup. "What about you? Were you and your ex-wife able to remain friends?"

"We're...not enemies." But they would be, if Kay wasn't in such sorry shape that he couldn't bring himself to ream her out for the mischief she'd wrought!

"So why couldn't you make it work between you?"

You're more married to that company of yours than you are to me, Mike D'Alessandro, and I'm tired of it. I have ambitions, too, and they amount to something more exciting

*than reading a set of blueprints. My talent's being wasted
in this backwater. You could still build award winning
houses if we moved to L.A.....*

*My work is here, Kay. You knew that when you married
me.*

And you knew I wanted a career in show business!

"We were looking for different things and ended up going in different directions to find them."

"It doesn't sound like much of a reason to end a marriage. Couldn't you have worked out a compromise?"

"Could you, when you saw your marriage going down
the tubes?" he snapped, irked by the implicit censure in
her question.

She held his gaze a moment. "I had more compelling
reasons to file for divorce which involved more than just
me and Todd. I had a baby to think about."

"Most people consider that a good reason to fight to save
a marriage."

"I did fight. For over five years. But it was a battle I
couldn't win."

"*Five years*? You mean to say, you and your ex were
having trouble before you adopted Jeremy?"

"Yes."

"Then what the hell right did you have to bring an innocent baby into the middle of it?"

His anger caught them both by surprise. He bellowed,
and she flinched. But the pink flush staining her cheeks told
him she'd asked herself the same question and suffered
agonies of guilt over the answer, which made it easier for
him to swallow his outrage and say, "Sorry, Camille. I
didn't mean to shout like that and I've got no business
judging you. I'm sure you thought you were acting in
everyone's best interests at the time."

She stared across the lawns to the sun-baked hills in the

distance. "I thought having a baby would improve things. I called him my miracle child. But he wasn't able to fix what had gone wrong. I suppose, when I realized that, I should have given him the chance to be adopted into a better home, with two parents who wanted him, instead of just one. But it would have broken my heart." She bit her lips, clamping down on them until they flattened into a thin line of misery. She closed her eyes, but not before he caught the sheen of tears. "I loved him so much—too much, some people might say. He's my whole life."

"I don't think a child can ever be loved too much," Mike said, feeling lower than dirt for raking up memories which caused her such obvious pain—but not enough that he could ignore the growing list of questions gnawing at his mind worse than an aching tooth. Damn it, if his boy had been bought to plug the holes in a leaking marriage, Kay wasn't the only one with a lot to answer for! He'd seen the agreement she'd signed and he didn't need to be a lawyer to know she'd been dazzled more by the money she stood to gain than any thought of what would be best for her baby. "And it's not as if he doesn't still have two parents."

"But he doesn't have two parents, Michael, that's the pity of it."

"Why not? Your ex isn't dead, is he?"

"No," she cried, "though, God forgive me, I sometimes wish he was!"

He'd slumped back into a corner of the swing, feigning the sort of mild interest a stranger might find in her story, but this latest turn in the conversation had him jackknifing to attention again. "Why?"

"Oh, it's a long, pathetic story, and not one you want to hear."

Wrong, sweetheart!

But it wouldn't do to appear too eager, so he forced himself to remark as casually as he knew how, "Why don't you let me be the judge of that?"

She made a face. "Todd has what's politely called 'a substance abuse problem.'"

"You mean, he's a lush?"

"To say the least."

Uh-oh! He didn't like where this was leading. "Are you saying he's into more than just booze?"

"Yes."

"Drugs?"

"I'm afraid so."

And you allow him unsupervised visits with my son?

How he didn't yell the words aloud, he hardly knew. He wanted to hit something. *Something?* Hell, he wanted to break every bone in Todd Whitfield's body! As for his son's adoptive mother…!

Bitterness welled up in him, so strong he could taste it, and this time it was directed at her. Did she have *any* brains behind that pretty face, any backbone at all? Afraid of what he might say, of the recriminations he was tempted to fling at her but which would blow his cover if he did, he lunged off the swing and strode up and down the length of the pool deck until he'd recovered enough control that he trusted himself to phrase his next question with a semblance of detachment. "I gather we're talking about more than the occasional aspirin for his hangovers? That he's into the illegal stuff?"

"Yes."

"And that doesn't worry you?"

"No. It's no longer my business or my concern." She wiped her fingers across her face and pushed her hair out of her eyes. "I'm not his baby-sitter. Not anymore."

But you're my son's, damn it!

He took a calming breath. "How the blazes do you leave a helpless child with a man like that and sleep at night, Camille? Or isn't that any of your concern, either?"

"Don't be ridiculous," she said. "I wouldn't let him within a mile of my son. Jeremy hasn't seen Todd since the day we went our separate ways. I doubt he even remembers he ever had a father."

The weight inside Mike's chest eased a little. "What if Todd suddenly decides he wants visitation rights?"

"I'd move heaven and earth to prevent it. But it won't happen. He relinquished all claim to Jeremy at the time of the divorce. I have his written promise that he'll never try to interfere in my son's life."

And if it was anything like the adoption agreement he'd drawn up, it wasn't worth the paper it was written on! "What guarantee do you have that he'll abide by such a promise?"

"We've been apart over two years, Michael, and he hasn't even phoned, let alone tried to come to my house. He no longer lives in California. I think that spells out pretty clearly that he's not interested in resuming any sort of relationship with his son. I can see from your face that you're having a hard time believing this, but if you'd lived with one, you'd know that addicts don't care about anything except their addictions."

"I know they can kick the habit and resume useful, productive lives if they put their minds to it. And it would seem to me that having a son I wasn't allowed to see would be incentive enough to stay clean."

"You're assuming Todd cares about Jeremy, but he doesn't."

"Then why the devil did he agree to the adoption?"

"Because he wanted me, and he thought, if he found a way to give me the baby I longed for, that he'd be able to keep me. He knew I was ready to leave him and he was desperate to give me a reason to make me stay.''

''So he bribed you by buying you a child?'' Try as he might, Mike couldn't keep the sneer out of his voice. ''Gee, what a novel concept! But I guess when a woman's got more money than she knows what to do with and a man wants to impress her, a string of pearls or a diamond ring don't cut much ice.''

''Is that the kind of person you think I am? Do you really believe I'm so selfish, so…*capricious* that I'd use *anyone*, let alone a helpless baby, like that?''

The stricken look she turned on him left him feeling as if he'd kicked a puppy, but the facts as she'd related them were pretty incriminating. ''If I'm missing something here,'' he said, hardening his heart against the misery she couldn't hide, ''clue me in. Because unless I've misunderstood, you knowingly stayed in a bad marriage just so you could get your hands on a child.''

Neither of them noticed they were no longer alone until her mother's voice cut across the conversation. ''I'm not sure by what right you feel justified in badgering my daughter like this, Mr. D'Alessandro, but since she's obviously too distressed to point out the obvious, I'll do it for her. Nothing about her life is any of your business. She owes you no explanations for the choices she's made, and if you had half the brains that you have brawn, you'd have arrived at that conclusion without my having to spell it out for you.''

''We're having a private conversation, Mrs. Younge,'' he snapped, in no mood to tolerate her insults on top of everything else. ''Take a hike!''

Vibrating with outrage, she scoffed, ''Private? I could hear every word coming out of your mouth the minute I stepped from my car. I imagine half the town could.''

"Oh, Mother, please!" Spots of color on her cheekbones heightened the pallor on Camille's face. She really did look about ready to keel over. "Stop exaggerating and don't interfere. Michael and I are having a perfectly harmless conversation."

"Really? Try telling that to Jeremy. He might be only three, Camille, but his hearing and eyesight are every bit as good as mine, and it might interest you to know that when I arrived, I found him watching you from the terrace."

Camille looked up at the house, her expression horrified. "I expected he'd still be napping. How long had he been there, do you think?"

"Long enough to ask me why Mr. D'Alessandro was making you cry."

"Damn!" Much though he hated to admit it, the old bat had a point. Judging from the little Camille had revealed, Mike guessed the boy had lived through enough emotional turmoil already, without his adding to it. "Camille, it might be best if I left."

"But we haven't finished—!"

"For once, I must agree with your guest." Her mother, bristling like a guard dog about to attack, stepped between him and Camille. Behind her, the pool glimmered turquoise in the sunlight. "You can find your own way out, I'm sure, Mr. D'Alessandro."

Oh, yeah! And one wrong step on my part, you over-bleached string bean, and you'd be in the water with your high-priced silk skirt floating up around your ears, and wouldn't that be something to see!

Grinning at the image he'd conjured up, he nodded at Camille. "I'm out of here. Thanks for the lunch."

"Will I see you again, Michael?"

"Not if your mother sees me first," he said. "*Sayonara!*"

CHAPTER FOUR

SOME twenty yards from Maddox Lodge, the guest house where Michael was staying, she found a place to park. A slight hollow only, it sloped away from the paved surface of the road at such a steep angle that when she backed into it, she feared for a moment that the car might flip over.

It served the purpose though. A bend in the lane behind hid her from anyone watching from the house. A stand of trees immediately ahead shielded her from an approaching vehicle yet allowed her to see the warning sweep of headlights turning off the main highway. Killing the engine, she settled down to wait.

It was almost nine-thirty, well over seven hours since she'd sent her mother packing, and almost eight since Michael had left. But it had taken most of the intervening time for Camille to find the courage to follow her instincts and go after him. She'd left Nori in charge at home, and driven to the guest house with her heart knocking against her ribs in nervous anticipation.

But, "He's not here," Susan Maddox had said, when she came to the door. "I haven't seen him since he left this morning."

"Left? You mean, he checked out?" The panic came out of nowhere, leaving Camille fighting for breath.

"No, all his stuff's still in his room. I just meant he's not here right now, which isn't unusual. He's gone most days and seldom gets back before dark." Susan had regarded her curiously. "You look a bit frazzled, Camille. Do you want me to have him call you when he gets in?"

She'd have said yes, if she'd thought he'd comply, but although the anger in his voice when he left her house that afternoon had been directed mostly at her mother, the disgust in his eyes he'd reserved solely for Camille. She thought it unlikely he'd initiate further contact.

"No, thanks," she'd said. "I'll wait and catch him later."

How much later, though, was the critical question. Whether it was instinct or fear she couldn't say, but something told her that his time in Calder was coming to an end, and the thought of his leaving filled her with inexplicable desolation.

Her mother would tell her she was crazy, and no doubt she must be, lurking in the dark like some third-rate private investigator on a stakeout, but she couldn't let him go, not yet, and certainly not with the way they'd left things that afternoon. Too many things remained unsaid between them, too much…emotion unexplored.

What kind of emotion, Camille? her rational self mocked. *And please don't tell me you're so far gone that you're deluding yourself into thinking you're in love with the man. If you're determined to make a fool of yourself, at least act your age and recognize lust when it's staring you in the face!*

Was that really what tonight's escapade boiled down to? Instead of being snug at home where she belonged, was she sitting in the dark waiting to accost a man who might well laugh at her—or worse, reject her outright—all because she was starving for a little male attention?

No, there was more at risk than that. Her integrity was on the line. Jeremy had seen and heard too much of that afternoon's exchange between her and Michael, and the conversation resulting from it hadn't been easy, not for Camille or for her son.

Why don't I have a daddy, Mommy?

Well, darling, some little boys just don't, that's all.

But Andrew has a daddy. He sleeps at their house all the time. Why can't I have one, too?

She'd tried to satisfy his curiosity by steering a middle road between outright lies and complete disclosure of a truth too sordid and complex for a child to grasp. But the task, coming so soon after Michael's probing interrogation, had left her with an urgent need to make the man, as well as the child, understand that she'd tried to act in everyone's best interests.

Michael D'Alessandro might be nothing more than a stranger passing through her life, but they shared something special and she would not soon forget him. The impressions he took away with him mattered to her a very great deal. She couldn't let him leave believing she was a selfish, unfit mother. She had to clarify to him, face-to-face, all the reasons why she'd felt justified in going ahead with the adoption. She only hoped he'd show more inclination to listen than he had when he'd stormed out of her house that afternoon.

And if he refused?

Her car, a roomy BMW 750, felt too close and confining suddenly. She opened the sunroof, lowered the seat to a full reclining position, then lay back and took deep breaths of the flower-scented air.

Of course he'd listen!

Night noises—the chirp of crickets, an owl's eerie call, a dog barking in the distance—competed with the nervous thud of her heart. Overhead, stars blanketed the sky and reflected pinpricks of light on the slack surface of the river. A lover's moon rose behind the trees.

And she, holed up in her car on the side of the road, sat waiting for a man who probably hadn't spared her a second thought since he'd marched out of her house that afternoon. If her mother knew what she was up to, she'd have her committed!

Folly on top of folly had been how Glenda Younge described Camille's behavior, during their confrontation earlier. "Explain to me, if you will, your fascination for a man about whom you know absolutely nothing but the most superficial details," she'd demanded, as the sound of Michael's car faded away. "What sort of hold does he have over you that you'd share with him confidential information about your marriage?"

At a loss, Camille had turned away. How could she explain something she didn't herself understand? To try, especially to someone of her mother's skeptical nature, was to invite nothing but ridicule.

As though regretting having spoken so bluntly, her mother had touched her shoulder. "Not that I care one iota what the man thinks of you, dear, but you must know that, to an outsider, your reasons for bringing Jeremy into your home appear self-serving, if not downright immoral! You've said yourself, often enough, that if you'd had the slightest inkling of the extent of Todd's problems, you'd never have gone ahead with the adoption."

"If Michael's so unimportant, why are you making such an issue of my associating with him?"

"Because both your father and I feel there's more to his being here than meets the eye, and we're worried by your willingness to let him into your life. Think about it, Camille! The man claims he's here on vacation, but even the most dedicated tourist can see everything Calder has to offer inside two days. So why do you suppose he's still hanging around over a week after he first showed up? More to the point, what's his real interest in you?"

"Maybe he likes my company."

"Or maybe he has a more devious agenda. It doesn't take a genius to see you're a wealthy woman. One look around at everything you have here…!" Graceful hands fluttering like doves, she'd gestured at the gardens, the pool, the house.

If she hadn't still been too close to tears, Camille might have laughed. "Is it so inconceivable to you that a man might want me for myself?"

"Of course not! But why this man? What does he hope to gain in making such a play for you when, by his own admission, he's just passing through the area? I know you think I'm overly critical and suspicious—"

"You're a snob, and we both know it."

"Perhaps so. But I'm also a mother who's afraid her daughter is being used and will end up being badly hurt—again! Whether or not you're willing to admit it, the divorce *did* leave you very vulnerable, Camille."

"At the time, yes. But it's been over two years now and I've recovered. Enough that I'm ready to resume a normal life."

"Normal's one thing!" Her mother's well-modulated voice had risen dramatically. "But stepping out with a man like Michael D'Alessandro, just because he's making himself available, is pure madness."

Oh, Mother, she thought, closing her eyes to the beauty of the night, *how would you react if I'd confessed that I'm in too deep to simply walk away? What would you say if I told you I'm already half in love with his smile, that his voice stirs my blood, and that with one kiss he melted the cold protective wall I'd built around my heart?*

The owl hooted again, a sleepy, hypnotic sound. The stars swam in the sky, their bright edges less sharply defined than they'd been a moment ago. A wisp of cloud hung over the moon. She found, if she stared at it long enough, that she could make out Michael's face in its shape.

Yes, there was the strong line of his jaw, the sweep of his cheekbones, the curve of his mouth....

He'd had enough for one day.

When he arrived at St. Mary's, Kay had barely known he was there. She'd opened her eyes once, smiled at him, and reached for his hand before sinking back into a sleep so closely imitating death that, if it hadn't been for the rhythmic leap of the pulse at her throat, he'd have thought she'd slipped away.

He'd remained with her well into the evening, the questions, the *accusations* he'd wanted to fling at her, vying with the pity he couldn't suppress. So he'd kept everything bottled up inside, along with the anger he'd brought with him from Camille's.

It was a deadly mix that stayed with him during the drive back to Calder, and he was in no mood to play good Samaritan when he saw the other car pulled so far over on the soft shoulder of the road that it was in imminent danger of sliding into the ditch.

He drove as far as the B and B, parked in his usual spot, grabbed the flashlight from the glove compartment, and headed back to investigate. If a couple were making out in the back seat, it was probably expecting too much to hope they still had their clothes on. But given the way his luck had been running lately, it was more likely he'd come across a body—some poor slob who'd maybe lost everything on the stock market and decided to end it all on a quiet country lane.

The moon cast just enough light for him to make out a top-of-the-line BMW with the sunroof open. To prevent the windows from steaming up? He didn't think so! The silence emanating from within the car was too deep. If there were occupants inside, they weren't moving around.

He approached the driver's door, aimed the flashlight's beam at the window, and let it play over the face of the woman stretched out behind the wheel. He hadn't known he'd been holding his breath until it blasted out of his lungs in shock.

What the hell…!

She wasn't moving. She lay flat on her back. One arm dangled between the front seats, the other was tucked out of sight beneath her body. But apart from the fact that her being there made absolutely no sense, what scared the living daylights out of him was that her legs were sprawled slackly apart in a way that would have had Mother Younge reaching for the smelling salts.

Something was very wrong. In fact, it looked to him as if she was unconscious.

Stepping closer, he rapped sharply on the window.

At first, she didn't know where she was. Was aware only of a chill on her skin, pins and needles in her hands and feet. And light, relentless and brilliant, scoring at her sleep-dazed eyes.

Then, in a rush, memory returned, and with it sudden stark fear. Beyond the aura of light outside her car, a figure loomed; a murky silhouette imprinted darkly against the fitful glow of the night sky.

She let out a shriek and scooted across to the passenger seat, one hand shielding her eyes, and the other searching for the door handle. But if there was no recognizing the face of the man peering in at her, nor was there any mistaking his voice.

"Camille? What the devil are you doing out here at this hour?"

"Waiting for you," she wheezed, clutching one fist to her racing heart. "What the devil are *you* doing spying on me like that? And will you please point that blasted light somewhere else before I go blind?"

He stepped back and directed the beam over her car. "I don't know who you paid to teach you to park," he said conversationally, "but either you should ask for a refund or else negotiate a few free lessons."

Oh, how like a man! "If you think I've been sitting here half the night for the pleasure of listening to you lecture me on my driving skills, think again! I had something a bit more important in mind."

"I'm sure you had, and heaven forbid I should be handing out unwanted advice." He was laughing at her, not outright perhaps, but it was there in his voice. "However, at the risk of being told it's none of my concern, your car appears to be listing dangerously to starboard. I suggest you drive up onto the road before we take this conversation any further—unless, of course, you prefer to conduct it from the bottom of the ditch?"

It occurred to her then that the car was sitting at an even steeper angle than it had been before, and as if to verify the fact, it gave a little lurch to the right. She braced her arm against the door and tried to sound nonchalant. "I think I might've left it too late."

He climbed back onto the road and took stock. She couldn't be certain, but she thought he was openly grinning. "Not if I give you a boost from behind," he decided. "Quit cowering over there and get back behind the wheel."

"And do what?"

No doubt about the grin this time; he was definitely having a good time at her expense. "Start the engine, honey child, what else? Then shift into low gear and step on the gas. Gently."

"It sounds too dangerous. What if I slide backward?"

He practically cackled aloud at that. "Then you'll have to scrape up my remains and your mother'll declare a national holiday to celebrate my early demise."

The car sighed gently and settled further into the unstable shoulder of the lane like a weary body sinking into a mattress. Through the open sunroof she heard gravel slithering out from under the wheels. "This is no time for jokes!" she said, her voice splintering with fright.

"And you're in no position to be giving me orders, Camille," he said calmly. "Trust me, together we can do this."

And together they did, though not before she felt the car skidding out of control and, in an effort to correct it, pressed her foot down hard on the accelerator.

A rooster tail of dirt spurted out from under the rear wheels. She heard a yell, felt pinpricks of sweat break out down her spine, and almost sheared off one of the trees ahead as the car shot out of the hollow and onto the pavement.

Legs shaking, blood pumping, she set the parking brake and climbed out. "Michael?"

But all the moon showed was an empty strip of road and, off to one side, the dark shape of a prostrate body.

"*Michael!*" She had no recollection of covering the distance between them. Felt no pain as she fell to her knees beside him. All her awareness was focused on her fingers sliding over the warm skin of his neck in search of a pulse, and the relief that flooded through her when she found it to be steady and strong.

He moved then, heaving himself onto all fours and hunching over with a muffled groan that lapsed into something which sounded suspiciously like retching.

"Are you throwing up?" she cried, envisioning all manner of internal injuries.

His eyes gleamed malevolently in the moonlight. "No, sweetheart. I'm trying to spit out the mouthful of dirt *your car* threw up when you stepped on the gas. I thought I made it clear that gunning the motor isn't a good idea when you're up to your hubcaps in sand and loose gravel?"

"I panicked," she said. "I thought the car was going to roll. I'm so sorry."

He ran an experimental finger over his mouth. "I guess I should be glad I still have all my teeth."

"Let me look at you."

They were kneeling so close that his shirt brushed the front of her blouse. Cupping his jaw, she turned his head from side to side. He hadn't shaved since that morning. Except for the silky line of an old scar just below his right ear, his skin had the texture of fine pumice against her fingertips. His eyelashes threw inky crescents of shadow over his cheekbones. And his mouth…. Oh, better not to dwell too long on his mouth!

"I don't see any blood," she said, "but you do have a scratch on your chin."

"No kidding!" His voice slid a husky octave lower than usual and his fingers closed around her wrist to imprison her hand against his cheek. "And what do you propose to do about it?"

The way he managed to infuse the question with outright invitation left her in no doubt about what he had in mind. His mouth was so close to hers, his words vibrated against her lips.

Sounding as if she'd been winded from a blow to the solar plexus, she said, "You want me to kiss it better?"

"Isn't that what mothers do best?"

"Not to grown men."

If she'd tried, she couldn't have found a more effective way to ruin the mood or the moment. "You're quite right," he said, hauling her upright and putting a safe six feet of space between them. "In that case, why don't we stop playing games, and you tell me why you were lying in wait for me to get back?"

She'd been so sure he was going to take her up on her first offer, so *ready* to throw caution and propriety to the winds and kiss him, that she could barely swallow her disappointment. "Oh…it's nothing really. I just thought, what with it's being such a lovely evening…so mild and all—"

"Camille, by your own admission you've been waiting half the night to speak to me, which leads me to expect it must be a matter of some importance to you and perhaps even to me, right?"

She nodded, miserably aware that she was making an utter fool of herself.

"Then don't expect me to buy the lame excuse that you wanted to chat about the weather." His gaze scoured her face in the moonlight. "What's really going on here?"

"I feel I owe you an apology. Not only was my mother very rude to you this afternoon but she interrupted us before I had the chance to explain—about my marriage to Todd and the reasons we adopted Jeremy. But it's a long, sordid story which you probably don't want to hear."

"Wrong. I've got nothing but time on my hands and I don't subscribe to the catchphrase 'never apologize and never explain.' I happen to believe confession is good for the soul."

"But it's all rather…personal."

"In my experience, anything to do with marriage generally is."

She sighed. "You're not going to let me off the hook, are you?"

"Not a chance." He took her elbow and steered her across the lane. "We'll walk down by the river. You might find it easier to talk if I'm not staring you in the face the whole time."

She thought it unlikely. Dredging up those painful memories was never easy. But doing so with the trees casting deep pools of shadow over the moon-splashed path at least made her feel less exposed.

"I guess," she began, "to put you fully in the picture, I should mention that Todd and I grew up in Calder. Our parents were good friends, belonged to the same clubs, supported the same charities, attended the same church. They were thrilled when we told them we wanted to get married and went out of their way to give us a fairy-tale wedding."

"Why don't we skip ahead to the reason you decided to adopt a child?" Michael said, with more than a touch of impatience. "I'm not a great fan of fairy tales."

"The point I'm trying to make is that we—Todd and I— thought we had it all. We were the golden children of golden parents—families with old money and social prestige to spare. We were rich, educated, socially aware, and beautiful in the sense that we were young and fit, with perfect teeth and shining hair and clear bright eyes."

"And then you found out that money couldn't buy love? You disappoint me, Camille. I expected you to come up with something more earth-shaking than that old cliché to explain your failed marriage. Is that why good old Todd started hitting the bottle?"

She glanced at him sharply, surprised by the bitterness in his tone. "No. That came much later, after years of trying to conceive a child."

"Uh-oh! Golden boy couldn't deal with a wife who couldn't lay the golden egg?"

"You know, Michael," she said, his sneering attitude

beginning to grate on her nerves, "I don't *owe* you this explanation, but since you insisted on hearing it anyway, the least you can do is keep the editorializing to yourself until I'm finished."

He stuffed his hands in his pockets and looked suitably chastened. "Point taken."

"I couldn't conceive. At least, that was the assumption for the first three years of our marriage. Finally, though, we went to a fertility specialist who diagnosed Todd as having...um...." She paused, searching for a delicate way to phrase the diagnosis. "The...*problem*."

Michael shared none of her diffidence. "Low sperm count, huh?" he said bluntly.

"Um...yes." She stared across the river to hide her discomfiture. "For the next two years, we tried without success every invention known to science in our desperate efforts to have a baby. Although I was disappointed, I believe Todd suffered more. You've never had children, Michael, so you might not think it all that important—"

He inhaled sharply and she tensed, expecting another derisive comment. But whatever he might have been inclined to interject, he thought better of it and said simply, "Go on."

"His inability to produce a son to carry on the family name took a terrible toll on his pride and self-esteem. Our relationship deteriorated. He changed. Closed himself off from me. Perhaps when a man is told he can't fertilize a woman's egg, he feels less like a man. Or perhaps what others viewed as unfortunate, Todd saw as shameful."

Afraid her voice would break as the memories came rushing back to haunt her, she lapsed into silence. "Take your time," Michael said, watching her. "I've got all night."

They strolled perhaps another hundred yards along the

riverbank before she felt able to pick up the thread of her story. "I don't pretend to have all the answers. I only know that he grew increasingly sullen and resentful, refused to seek help, refused to consider adoption, and refused to discuss ways of dealing with this crushing disappointment."

"Cripes, talk about spineless!"

Force of habit had her defending Todd, even after all this time. "Until you've tried to father a child yourself, Michael, you're hardly in a position to pass judgment!"

The breath hissed between his lips as though it was all he could do to hold on to his temper. "I don't have to be in his place to recognize the man was missing a few neurons if he couldn't figure out you were in as much pain as he was!"

"I don't know why you're getting yourself into such a state," she said. "I'm the one who had to live with him."

"Which prompts me to ask the obvious. Why the devil didn't you leave him?"

"When things reached the point where I was afraid of him, I did."

"If you're saying you waited until he started smacking you around before you took action, Camille, don't expect me to smile and slobber sympathy all over you. He might have made you his victim, but you're the one who let him get away with it."

"He never laid a hand on me. He took out his frustrations in other ways, drinking too much, driving too fast, being verbally aggressive with other people. He channeled all his energy into a controlled rage which was eating us both alive and I'd finally had enough. I told him I wanted a separation."

"And?"

"It did what no amount of pleading or persuading had managed to do. It seemed to be the shock that brought him to his senses. He begged for another chance, promised he'd clean up his act. And for a while, he did. Some of his old sweetness returned. I believed we were back on track, especially when, for the first time ever, he agreed to look into adopting and made good on the promise within weeks by finding a child for us.''

''And you weren't made the least bit suspicious by the speed with which he managed to do that? Where I come from, adoptions take months, sometimes years.''

''I was surprised at how quickly a baby became available, but Todd's a lawyer and he had connections. He put out the word and because we had the money to pay for a private adoption, I guess we were able to cut a few corners.''

''More than you can possibly know,'' Michael muttered, glaring ahead and striding along at a furious pace.

She raced to keep up with him. ''What's that supposed to mean?''

''Damned lawyers thinking they can bend the rules to suit their own ends, that's what it means!''

''We didn't do anything illegal, if that's what you're implying.''

''Are you sure? Did you read the fine print before you signed the adoption papers?''

''There was no fine print. We had a straightforward agreement drawn up which we and the birth mother signed, with Todd's two law partners acting as witness.''

''Didn't it strike you as odd that an important part of the equation was missing?''

''The natural father, you mean? He forfeited any rights he might have had when he walked out on his pregnant wife and left her to fend for herself.''

''Even if he were as delinquent as you seem to think, I

suspect you needed his signed permission for the agreement to hold up in court.''

"There's no 'even if' about it, Michael,'' she snapped. "The man was a louse and there isn't a court in this land who'd uphold his bid to contest the adoption, especially not after all this time.''

"There might be,'' he countered. "Given the fact that your husband opted out of the parental responsibilities he voluntarily undertook and then abandoned, a court might look very favorably on the natural father's claim to his blood child.''

"He'd have to get by me first and if you think I'd hand Jeremy over without a fight, you greatly underestimate the power of a mother's love! And whose side are you on, anyway?''

"I wasn't aware I was being asked to take anyone's side but if I had to choose, I'd say Jeremy's. Shouldn't the best interests of a child always take precedence over everything else?''

"Of course they should! Do you think I'm not aware, with every passing day, that Jeremy deserves two parents, that he *needs* a father? Don't you think, if I could, I'd give him one?'' She didn't know she'd begun to cry until her words choked on a sob. "But what do you expect me to do, Michael? Run out and shanghai the first man who slows down long enough for me to catch him, and force him to be a daddy to my boy?''

"No.'' He caught her hands and tried to pull her into his arms. "And I didn't mean to make you cry, either.''

"Don't you touch me!'' she cried, slapping his hands away. "You've left it a bit too late to play the sympathetic friend. I must have been mad to think I could confide in you or expect that you'd understand.''

"Hey," he said urgently, pinioning her wrists against his chest, "I'm not the enemy here, Camille."

But the reassurance came too late. His questions had raised specters she couldn't ignore.

How do we know the father won't show up one day, Todd? What if he decides he wants his baby, after all?

He won't.

How can you be sure?

Because I know what I'm doing. That agreement is watertight.

But you're the one who's always said there's no such thing as a contract which can't be broken.

I'm the legal expert, Camille, not you, so instead of harping on about things you know nothing about, why don't you stick to what you do best and look after the kid?

She'd let herself be convinced, in part because she had bigger things to worry about. Her husband's growing indifference toward their new son suggested that acquiring a baby had mattered more to Todd than being a father. Then the drinking started again, and with it the rages and the accusations.

What the natural father might or might not do had paled beside the very real risk to which she was exposing her son by remaining in such a marriage, and by the time she'd finally put her house in order again, her other fears lay so far in the past that she'd grown complacent.

Until Michael D'Alessandro came on the scene, that was, and unearthed them again!

"You might not be my enemy, but you're not my friend, either," she said, too overwrought to care that she was thrashing around in his arms like a wild thing. "If you were, you wouldn't be trying to undermine my confidence like this. I'm a good mother and I love my son."

"I know, I know! For Pete's sake, Camille, no one who's

seen you with Jeremy could ever doubt that and I never meant to suggest otherwise. Please stop crying, sweetheart.''

''I really don't know why I started.'' She leaned her head against his chest, all the fight suddenly seeping out of her. ''It's just that I sometimes feel I let Rita down and if she knew, she'd regret having trusted me with her baby. I promised her we'd give Jeremy what she couldn't give him—two parents and a loving, stable home. Yet within months of his birth, I'd filed for divorce and Todd had walked out of our lives for good.''

''You did what any mother would have done in the same situation. You protected your child the only way you could. Don't beat yourself up because Todd didn't hold up his end of the bargain. That was his choice, not yours.''

His voice flowed over her, deep and smoky, blunting all the rough edges of her distress. His arms closed around her, warm and strong. She had never felt so safe and protected.

''If I'd been married to a man like you to begin with,'' she said, lifting her face to his, ''things would have turned out differently.''

''Oh, yes,'' he said thickly. ''That much I can safely guarantee.''

She thought, from the way he spoke, that there might be a hidden message in his words. She thought, from the way he looked at her, that something was troubling him. She opened her mouth to ask him. But before she could voice the question, he bent his head and kissed her. And once again, everything fled her mind but the sheer magic of his lips on hers.

CHAPTER FIVE

HE TASTED of grass and the wildflowers that grew along the side of the road; of the river-scented air and the cool star-filled night. A dizzy, intoxicating mixture that left her so light-headed she sank against him with a whimper.

She wound her arms around his waist. Pressed herself so close that his belt buckle gouged the thin fabric of her dress. Driven by a raging hunger to know him ever more intimately, she let her hand slip down to caress his buttocks. Tilted her hips to meet the thrust of his.

He tore his mouth free and shoved her away so abruptly she'd have stumbled if he hadn't caught her. "This is madness! Get back in your car and go home."

"Why?" she asked him. "What are you afraid of?"

"Me," he said unsteadily.

"I'm not." She dared to touch him again, tracking the thin line of his scar with her forefinger. "I trust you."

"Never trust a stranger, Camille. You're asking for trouble if you do."

"Then let me rephrase it. I trust myself, and my instincts tell me you're a good and decent man."

"We both know your instincts aren't always on target. If they were, you'd never have married Todd."

She let her hand skim to the pulse throbbing at the base of his throat. "What's happening between us has nothing to do with Todd, Michael, and we both know it."

"It has nothing to do with anything!" he said savagely. "That's why, if you're a tenth as smart as you like to think you are, you'll get the hell out of here as fast as you can."

"I'll do that just as soon as you tell me you don't want to kiss me again."

"I don't want to kiss you again."

"Really?" She moved close enough that their bodies brushed against each other, and lifted her face to his. And waited.

The air whistled past his lips. "*Damn* you!"

The curse caressed her like a benediction, fraught with pent-up longing. It was all the encouragement she needed to continue along a course already so far beyond her usual diffidence that she wondered where she'd found the courage to set out on it in the first place. "Yes," she whispered, her lips feathering over his. "Damn me."

He hauled her into his arms. His body slammed against hers, powerful, unyielding, primitive. But his mouth…oh, his mouth wooed her with refined genius! She dissolved beneath its seduction. The moon could have fallen into the river and she wouldn't have cared. He held her spellbound.

"You're driving me crazy," he rumbled, the tip of his tongue teasing the outer shell of her ear, then plunging deep into the tightly furled inner coil—in and out, in and out, in bold imitation of sexual intimacy.

"Me, too," she said on a dying breath.

He threaded his fingers through her hair and cradled the back of her head in the palm of his hand. "The first time we kissed," he said, his gaze devouring her face, "I promised myself it would be the last."

"Why, when we do it so well?"

"Because I knew it would never be enough. And I was right. I want to make love to you, Camille." He slid his hand down her spine and splayed his fingers over the curve of her hip. His thumb stole into the crease of her groin, teasing, tantalizing. Swept a fleeting caress across the top

of her thigh and circled that part of her already weeping
for his touch, marking it his to possess.

A spasm of pleasure, so acute and unexpected that she
gasped aloud, quivered through her. Shamelessly, she im-
prisoned his hand between her thighs. "I wish you would!"

"No, you don't, not if you stop to think about it," he
said hoarsely. "We're neither of us the one-night-stand
type. Allowing ourselves to get carried away only serves
to make everything more complicated between us."

He might be refuting her assertion verbally, but the sin-
uous pressure of his hand against her susceptible flesh conveyed quite a different message. He could easily have broken the contact and left her wilting with disappointment,
but he didn't.

"You're making all the right noises, Michael," she said,
"but if you really believed what you're saying, you'd push
me away, just as you did the other night. You'd belittle me,
tell me I'm a tramp...."

His fingers curved to fit the shape of her more snugly.
"If I were to say that, would you make me stop what I'm
doing?"

He was stealing her soul, her mind, her sensibility.
"No...! Please, Michael...make love to me...."

He lifted his head and scanned the area, his breathing as
tortured as hers. "Not here. There's a place farther along
the river...." He stopped and pinned her in one last searching gaze. His mouth skimmed the planes of her face. "If
you're going to change your mind, Camille, now's the time
to say so."

Without hesitation, she placed her hand in his.

His fingers closed around hers, strong and dependable.
He led the way down the embankment and along the grassy
strip running beside the water to a stretch of sand half hidden by an overhanging willow. A shaft of moonlight

pierced the branches, just enough to show his heaving chest. Just enough to reveal the pale line of his scar against the darker shadow of his jaw. Just enough that she could see the swollen profile of his virility straining against the fly of his jeans.

She placed her hand flat against his waist, then drew it down in provocative slow motion until her palm covered him. He smothered a moan, but apart from the slow droop of his eyelashes, he remained perfectly still.

She slid her hand again to his waist, tugged free the hem of his T-shirt, and lifted it to bare his midriff. Although ridged with underlying muscle, his skin felt smooth; warm and pulsing with hidden energy.

She raised the hem higher. Moonlight played over the contours of his chest, creating a subtle patchwork of copper and bronze and mahogany. Too mesmerized by the symmetrical beauty of him to care what he might think of her daring, she leaned forward and swirled her tongue first over one flat nipple, and then the other.

Another strangled moan escaped him. Yet still, he didn't move.

She stroked her hands down the line of his ribs. Dropped to her knees and dipped her tongue into the hollow of his navel.

She had gone too far. The sky tilted, the willow tree swung at a crazy angle. With a soft thump, the ground tumbled up to meet her. Cool grainy sand clung to the back of her legs and speckled her hair. His body covered hers. The tough, male weight of him flattened the breath from her lungs. The feel of him, hard and pulsing with life, left her body aching and her mind spinning.

"Enough!" he muttered roughly.

But the hand pinning her wrists above her head was gentle; the knee inching her legs apart questing rather than encroaching.

For the space of a heartbeat or two, he scrutinized her, feature by feature. Then reining in a breath, he said, ''Don't push me to the brink too soon, Camille. If we're going to do this, let me show you at leisure what loving's all about.''

She squirmed beneath him, her blood churning at the promise she heard in his voice. Todd had never spoken to her in words charged with such impassioned restraint; never made her tremble with a single telling glance. From the earliest days of their marriage, their coming together had been all about reproduction. A matter of timing and technique.

''Your dress is lovely,'' Michael said, releasing her hands and pulling himself up to kneel astride her. ''Fine, just like you.'' He slipped the top button loose, then the next and the next, until only the gauzy half-cups of her bra covered her breasts. ''Fine and feminine,'' he said, pushing the dress down her arms and sliding the bra straps from her shoulders, ''just like you.''

A breath of river air drafted over her exposed skin and left goose bumps in its wake. He seared them into oblivion with his tongue, then fastened his mouth over the aching bud of her nipple.

A live wire of electricity raced from the point of contact to her pelvis, swift, sharp and exquisitely painful. She clutched at him, her nails gouging the smooth muscle of his shoulders. Her legs jerked spasmodically. ''Michael....'' she whimpered.

He reared back, peeled off his T-shirt, and tossed it behind him. It floated in the night, a white ghostly object drifting aimlessly a moment before dropping with a sigh into the long sweet grass at the foot of the willow.

Rising up to meet him, she fumbled with his belt. He

caught her hand and drew her to her feet. "No," he said, stepping back the better to watch her as she stood there, half undressed, with grains of sand sliding over her skin and trickling from the ends of her hair. "Get rid of the dress and the underwear, instead."

Hypnotized by his dark unblinking stare, she obeyed, moving as if she were in a trance. She kicked off her shoes and he, her partner in the surrealistic mating ritual, did the same with his. He shed his jeans at the exact moment that her dress puddled around her ankles; shucked off his briefs as she shed her panties.

Realizing she was staring, she half turned away. "If you can't even bring yourself to look at me," he said, "then you're not ready to have me make love to you, either."

Shyly, she ventured a glance at him. He stood naked before her, carved in moonlight and dusted with shadow; powerful and magnificent in his masculinity.

She had no recollection of how they came to be standing only a few inches apart. Did he move first? Did she? Or did involuntary strands of magnetism draw them together until his breathing mingled with hers and she could taste him deep in her lungs?

He touched his forefinger to her chin. Traced a thin line down her throat. Wove a tormenting figure eight around her breasts without actually touching them. Paused and said, "I knew you would be beautiful," then meandered down to draw a convoluted pattern from her ribs to her waist.

The shivering anticipation he left behind puckered her skin in a thousand places, tightening each pore until it shrieked for relief. "Ahh!" she cried helplessly, struggling to tame his elusive seduction, to halt his slow destruction of her soul.

He framed her hips in his hands. Steered her an inch

closer, just enough that the heated tip of him nudged at her belly. She teetered toward him, felt his kiss feather along her cheek and over her mouth, teasing, tempting. Felt his palm drift to the small of her back, and over the slope of her hip. His finger slipped between her thighs and pressed against her once. Just once.

A tiny scream tore loose from her throat. A tiny flood pooled where he'd touched. And a need measureless as the universe took hold of her, driving away whatever timidity she had left. She looped a frantic arm around his neck and reached down to touch him; to delight in the virile satin-smooth dimensions that made him a man.

He inhaled sharply and bore her to the sand once again. Covered her breasts with his big powerful hands. Left the damp imprint of his kisses down her rib cage and kept on going…lower and lower still.

A sliver of doubt clouded her mind. *Nice girls don't do this!*

But she'd left girlhood behind years before, and her thighs had a mind of their own. They parted willingly to accept him because they knew what she was only just coming to understand: that there was no reason to refuse him when all he wanted was to give her pleasure.

And give he did, with dedicated, exquisite finesse, inciting her to such delirium that she thought she'd splinter apart.

Finally, though, even his formidable self-discipline reached breaking point. Aligning his body with hers, he slipped his hands beneath her hips to forge an intimacy of flesh which allowed for no secrets between them, and with one masterful stroke invaded her. Driven by a pagan hunger, he rocked within her, awakening a deep, dark center that nothing and no one had touched before.

Caught in the ever more urgent rhythm of his loving, she

relinquished herself to its cadence. She heard him call out her name on an agonized breath, a warning in itself that he was losing his grip on sanity. His heart hammered next to hers, fierce and frantic. Obedient to every nuance of his loving, the tension spring coiling through her blood tightened in response. For one eternal second, every last inch of her—from her toes, to the backs of her knees, to her scalp—hung in the balance.

Then, with one last mighty thrust, he let his seed run free inside her, hot and robust. At that the earth dropped away, a sneaky trapdoor hurling her into a primeval free fall which would surely have destroyed her had his arms not held her safe. Battered by wave upon wave of sensation, she clung to him, the passion sweeping over her with a vengeance so completely foreign that she cried aloud in shock, a reedy, needy wailing that hung in the night like a banshee's call.

When its last echo faded away and the silence covered them again, Michael rolled to his side and tucked her into the curve of his body. He stroked his hand over her hair and down her arm.

So this, she thought dazedly, *is how it feels to be desired by a man for no reason other than the simple joy of giving his partner pleasure!*

"I can hear your mind buzzing. What are you thinking about?" he asked, his voice vibrating against her forehead.

"Nothing," she said, for how did a woman describe the wonder of her first orgasm, especially to a man who wasn't her husband? How did she begin to do justice to the purity of the experience, to the absolute sense of connection she'd felt with him, and not send him running for the hills by straying into the dangerous language of love?

"No regrets?"

"None."

His chest heaved in a silent sigh.

Disquieted, she said, "Are *you* having second thoughts, Michael?"

"About lying here in the buff where anyone might find us, and keeping you up long past your bedtime?" He attempted a laugh and disengaged himself from her. "Yes. You need to get home."

"Oh…!" Brimming with dismay, the exclamation was out before she could contain it. "You wish we hadn't…done it."

He wouldn't look at her and he didn't speak. Instead, he climbed into his clothes with unflattering speed and went to retrieve the flashlight which had rolled down by the water. Embarrassed, she took advantage of the momentary privacy to step into her panties and pull her dress over her head. Miserably aware of the damp sand sticking to her skin, of her utter dishevelment, she struggled to hang on to her dignity and not give way to the humiliation and disappointment threatening to burst free.

How could he so easily dismiss something she'd found beautiful beyond compare?

The answer hammered at her without a shred of remorse. *Because, stupid, it didn't mean anything at all to him!*

"If you're worried that I'm going to make a nuisance of myself and start stalking your every move, don't be," she said, striving to sound blasé. "I might not be the one-night-stand kind, as you so charmingly phrased it, but that doesn't mean I'm planning to boil your pet rabbit, either! There are no strings attached to what happened between us tonight."

He rotated the flashlight between his hands and expelled another sigh. "That's not what's worrying me."

But it was. Why else would he be in such a hurry to get rid of her?

''Well, you were very *good,* if that's what you're wondering.''

He didn't need to tell her he found the remark both uncalled-for and distasteful. Even in the semidark, the reproach on his face was unmistakable. ''I'll walk you to your car, Camille.''

''No need.'' She stuffed her feet into her sandals and fumbled with the buttons on her dress. But she was trembling so hard, she couldn't coordinate her fingers.

''I said, I'll walk you to your car.''

''And then what? Kiss me good-night and tell me you'll give me a call one of these days, when we both know you've no intention of doing any such thing? I'll pass, thanks!''

He ran his hand back and forth over the flashlight as though he hoped, if he rubbed it hard enough, a genie might appear and vaporize her in a puff of smoke. ''Are you always like this after you've—?''

''Had sex with a stranger?'' She pushed distraught fingers through her hair, scarcely aware of what she was saying. ''I really don't know. It's not something I've done before and I'm beginning to understand why. It's not worth the humiliation that follows.''

''I gave you every chance to back out before things went too far.''

''So you did. Chalk it up to inexperience that I didn't have the good sense to take you up on the offer, and rest assured I've learned my lesson. I made a mistake and I'm very sorry that you have to bear the brunt of my regret.''

He studied his feet, the overhanging branches of the willow tree, and finally, with marked reluctance, her face. ''I'm the guilty party here, Camille, not you. I hold myself entirely responsible for what happened tonight.''

Teeth clenched against the pain spearing her, she said,

"Spare me your charity, please! My pride's taken enough of a beating."

"The last thing I ever wanted was to hurt you."

"Perhaps," she said, furious to find her voice water-logged with tears. "But it happened anyway, which just goes to show that the road to hell really is paved with other people's good intentions."

He made a move toward her, hands outstretched, though whether in irritation or remorse she couldn't tell. All she knew was she couldn't bear to have him touch her again, not if she wanted to hang on to the crumbling edges of her composure—and hang on to it she must, if she was ever to look herself in the mirror again and not blush with shame at what she saw staring back.

Clutching the top of her dress closed, she stumbled away, up the bank and back along the lane to where her car sat ready to go at the turn of a key. Having to ask Michael D'Alessandro for help getting it back on the road—or worse, being forced to accept a ride home from him—would have been the last straw.

Where he was concerned, she'd made fool enough of herself to last a lifetime. She never wanted to see him again.

The squeal of tires split the silence. The smell of burning rubber chased away the scent of her still teasing his senses, and filled his mind with horror pictures.

Her car was powerful, designed for speed. She was angry and hurt and probably crying. And she was driving much too fast. If she ended up wrapped around a tree, or flew off the bridge a mile up the road and nose-dived into the river, it would be his fault.

Congratulations, jackass! You've really screwed up this time!

Furious with himself, he aimed a vicious kick at the willow tree. Pain exploded in his ankle and swept in jarring waves up his leg.

Too bad you didn't nail your head instead—or the other place you left your brains tonight!

Hopping around on his good foot, he cursed the day he'd agreed to Kay's request. Ignorance *was* bliss, and never mind what the pundits decreed. He'd been better off not knowing. Trouble was, now that he did, there was no going back. From the minute he'd learned he had a son, his life had been divided into two separate eras. Before. And after.

Something wrapped itself around his shoe, almost tripping him. When he bent to investigate, he found her bra tangled in the laces of his runner. ''Well, why the hell not?'' he muttered bitterly, shaking sand out of the flimsy half-cups and looping the straps over his fingers. ''I've stamped all over her pride already. Might as well grind a little dirt into her clothes as well, while I'm at it.''

But the only real dirt was that sticking to his conscience. He'd used her, pure and simple, to satisfy his own raging desire, and the worst of it was, he couldn't bring himself to regret it. She was lovely, and innocent in a way that had caught him so thoroughly off guard that he'd found himself dangerously moved. He'd known he should stop; that he couldn't afford to muddy his own agenda by losing his objectivity. And he'd known she would be incapable of maintaining hers.

It would have been different if she'd been cut from the same cloth as her mother. Then, he might have been able to tell himself that, sometimes, a man had to do what a man had to do—and believe it. But if Glenda Younge was as tough as old rope, Camille was delicate as a butterfly.

She'd been badly scarred by her marriage. He suspected that, until tonight, she'd never been with any other man but her husband. He was afraid the only way she'd forgive herself for what she'd done with him was to invest the incident with more meaning than it merited.

He'd heard it in her voice, in the quivering disappointment she hadn't been able to disguise. He'd seen it in the way she'd bitten her lip and scrunched her eyes closed to stop herself from bursting into tears when he hadn't told her what she'd hoped to hear. But what scared him the most was how badly he'd wanted to chase after her and restore her illusions; to give her the fairy-tale ending she was looking for.

"Get a grip!" he admonished himself scornfully, stuffing the bra into his back pocket and heading up the bank to the road. "This isn't high school and she's not the cheerleader who let you get into her pants because you're too full of raging hormones to control yourself! She's the mother of your child. If you really care about her, do the decent thing and get the hell out of her life now, before you cause any more damage."

Trouble was, he couldn't do that. He was in too deep to walk away. And that was the real reason he practically gagged on the bitter aftertaste of guilt souring his tongue.

The morning after, she'd told Fran, *Don't bother playing matchmaker anymore. The Michael D'Alessandro experiment was a disaster. I never want to see him again.*

She'd told herself it was true, that he was a louse who'd wormed his way into her affections by being kind to Jeremy, that she was a dreadful judge of character to have been so easily taken in by a pair of broad shoulders and a charming smile, and that she was lucky she'd found out early what sort of man he really was: a bounder who preyed on a woman's susceptibility to clever seduction.

So it made not a scrap of sense that when, five days after *it* had happened, he showed up on her doorstep again and started out with, "I'm probably the last person you want to see, but—"

He looked a little drawn, as if he, too, had had trouble sleeping. But the shadows under his eyes did nothing to detract from his beauty. He was gorgeous in navy linen pants and a pale blue shirt topped with a lightweight beige jacket. It wasn't fair that he should catch her looking so pale and uninteresting!

Curbing the urge to fling herself into his arms and thank him for coming back, she said coolly, "Correct me if I'm wrong, but didn't we already play this scene last week?"

At least he had the grace to look sheepish. "I'm too embarrassed to come up with a more creative opening, Camille. The fact is, you've been on my mind ever since the other night. I never should have let things go so far."

"It's a bit too much after-the-fact for regrets, don't you think? The damage has been done."

"Perhaps, but that doesn't mean I can just dismiss it. I need to know that you're all right."

"And it took you this long to figure that out?" She'd promised herself she wouldn't betray how devastated she'd been by his neglect, but the hurt came tumbling out the minute she opened her mouth. "It's been nearly a week, Michael. If you really cared about me, you wouldn't have waited this long to try to make amends."

"I'd have been in touch sooner, but other…business came up."

"Of course. And business always comes before pleasure." She didn't care that she sounded like a fishwife. He was lucky she didn't rake her nails down his handsome face!

"The point is, it *was* a pleasure."

"For you, perhaps."

"I thought, at the time, for both of us."

She cringed before his unflinching honesty. Whatever else his omissions, he'd given her a gift she'd always cherish and she did them both an injustice by pretending otherwise.

The truth was, all those times she and Todd had tried so hard to make a baby, a part of her had remained aloof and refused to abdicate control. She'd never had an orgasm in her life, but she'd read enough to convince herself she knew what they were all about—until the other night when reality had made a mockery of her attempts to fool anyone, least of all herself.

"Was I wrong, Camille?"

She wished she could lie, and knew she never could. Not to him. "No."

Some of the tension went out of his shoulders. "Then can we start over and this time try to remain nothing more than friends?"

Could they? Would friendship be enough, after what they'd shared? On the other hand, could anything be worse than the terrible emptiness she'd known when she thought she'd lost him forever? "I don't know," she said. "But it's a chance I'm willing to take."

CHAPTER SIX

His sudden smile washed away all the hurt and anger she'd nourished over the last few days. "Thank you. That's more than I dared hope for and a lot more than I deserve."

"Not really. What happened between us the other night...." Her mouth went dry but she held his gaze. "We both know I was a willing accomplice, Michael, if not the downright aggressor. If I didn't like the outcome, I've got only myself to blame."

"Let's leave blame out of it," he said, mesmerizing her all over again with the way his lips shaped the words. As if it had happened only minutes before, the memory of how he'd used that mouth to drive her wild flashed to the forefront of her mind, evoking a jolt of sensation that left her trembling inside. "I've got enough on my conscience without adding blame to the list. Let's settle for 'memorable', instead."

Amazed at how quickly the right man saying the right words could make the world lose all its ugliness and restore a woman's faith in herself, Camille opened the door wider. "Would you like to come in? It's a bit early for lunch, but we can have coffee. Nori's taken Jeremy to the park so it's nice and peaceful around here for a change."

"Thanks, but I can't. I have a pressing appointment in the city, and I'm already running late."

Another one? Good grief, with the amount of time he spent in San Francisco, why didn't he just stay there as well and save himself a lot of unnecessary driving? Unreasonably disappointed, she said, "You shouldn't have bothered to stop by then. You could just as easily have phoned.''

"And take the coward's way out?'' He shook his head. ''I might not always do the right thing, but I hope I'm man enough to apologize face-to-face when I've made a mistake. In any case, I had to return this.''

Reaching into his jacket pocket, he pulled out a small plastic bag bearing the Maddox Lodge logo and dropped it in her hand. Weighing no more than an ounce or two, it rustled lightly against her palm.

"Oh!'' She realized at once what it was, and hardly knew where to look. "My bra. How embarrassing! Imagine if someone else had found it.''

"No one else did, Camille. I made sure of that. And if I'd known I was going to make you blush like this, I just might have mailed it to you, instead of presenting it in person.''

He was teasing her, beguiling her all over again with his smile and the laughter in his eyes. She covered her burning cheeks with her hands. "I'm being ridiculous, aren't I?''

"Not a bit. 'Ridiculous' is the last word I'd apply to you.'' As quickly as it had arisen, his amusement died. "Unless you have other plans, will you have dinner with me tomorrow night?''

"If you like.'' Her answer, embarrassingly overeager, was out almost before he'd finished the question.

"I'd like,'' he said. "When shall I pick you up?''

"It's better for me if we make it later—say half past eight? That way, I'll have time to give Jeremy his bath and read him a bedtime story before I leave.''

"Eight-thirty it is. See you then.''

For a second, he sort of hovered on the doorstep, as though uncertain how to take his leave. With a hug? A peck on the cheek?

She wouldn't have minded either one. He'd gone a long way toward redeeming himself by coming to her house and being so frank. In the end, though, she was left wanting. He stepped away, gave a little salute, then took off down the steps to his car without a backward glance.

She told herself not to read more into his visit than he'd intended. He'd made it clear where they stood, that the most he could offer was friendship, and probably the only reason he'd asked her to dinner at all was that he felt he owed it to her to make up for their last meeting. She'd be a half-wit to imagine for one second that he harbored any romantic intentions toward her.

"Maybe so," she said, watching until he was lost to sight by the shrubbery lining the driveway, "but just in case, I'll spring for a new dress this time."

"For someone who said she never wanted to see the man again, you're going to extraordinary lengths to impress him," Fran remarked, lounging on the little sofa reserved for guests in *Hyacinthe,* Calder's most upscale ladies' boutique. "That must be the tenth outfit you've modeled, which suggests to me that, for you at least, there's a lot more riding on this dinner date than a decent meal and a good-night handshake."

"I asked you to come shopping with me because I value your fashion judgment, not to listen to you playing pop psychologist," Camille said, adjusting the scarf of the silk crepe two-piece she'd tried on. "What do you think of this?"

"Get rid of it. You look like the mother of the bride with a slingshot hanging around her neck." Shuddering, Fran got up and rifled through a rack of newly-arrived designer creations which Camille had dismissed as being dressier than the occasion called for. "Ah, *yes!*" she crowed, holding up a shimmery beaded number with a plunging neckline and a thigh-high slit up the front of the narrow skirt. "This, on the other hand, was tailor-made for you."

"Fran, it's indecent!"

"On me, maybe. On you, it'll merely look decadent. Come on, Camille, at least try it on. What've you got to lose?"

"Common sense, that's what—something I don't seem to have much of where Michael's concerned! Wearing a dress like that is just asking for trouble."

Fran shook the thing like a matador trying to goad a reluctant bull to action with his cape. "You've got the legs to carry it off, dearie, and Michael strikes me as a very civilized man. I doubt he's going to attack you between the soup and salad course just because you're showing a bit of skin."

"*No!* It's too...formal. We're having dinner, not attending the governor's ball."

But the more she looked, the more she weakened, and Fran knew it. "Let's see how it looks on you before we decide."

Why fight the inevitable, especially since nothing else had caught her fancy? "All right, but I'm telling you now, it's a waste of time."

It wasn't, though. It was a dream come true. The silk lining shimmied over her body like a caress. The silver-blue beading echoed the color of her eyes. The lightly-boned bodice meant she could dispense with a bra and wouldn't have to worry about straps showing. The slit in the skirt tempted a little, without revealing too much. In short, the dress was perfect.

"You'll knock his socks off," Fran decreed, when Camille appeared for inspection. "Get out your credit card and prepare to blow your budget, girlfriend. We've found the killer dress for the occasion.''

Although he managed to keep his socks on when she opened the door to Michael at thirty-two minutes past eight that evening, he *did* look as if someone had knocked the wind out of him. "Holy cow!" he wheezed, his gaze skating past the daring neckline to the slit in her skirt. "That is some outfit!"

"Should I take that to mean you approve?"

He blinked and ventured another hurried glance at the way the fabric barely managed to drape her breasts. "Oh yeah! I just wish I did you credit as your date, is all! As it is, you're stuck with what you see."

What she saw was so delectable, her mouth watered. He wore a silver-gray jacket over a white dress shirt whose French cuffs were held closed by discreet silver links. His dark gray tie gleamed with the subtle sheen of fine Italian silk. The knife-edge crease in his black dress pants bisected the top of hand-made black leather shoes. In her book, he easily topped the list of best-dressed men-about-town, and there wasn't a thing about him she wanted to change.

Curbing her enthusiasm for fear it might send him running for the hills, she said primly, "You look very nice."

He gave a wry laugh. "Kind of you to say so. Now that we've got all that out of the way, let's go."

"Would you like to come in for a drink, first?"

"No, thanks." He reared back as if she'd made an indecent proposition. "I managed to get us in at the Quail Lodge which I'm told is a good half hour's drive from here, and whoever took the booking made it pretty clear they won't hold our table if we're late."

"I'm surprised you were able to get a reservation at all," she said, but it was a lie. He could charm apples off trees without even trying, and there wasn't a woman alive who wouldn't succumb to the sexy timbre of his voice sliding down the phone.

"How's Jeremy?" he asked, once they'd cleared the town limits and were headed east. "Still thrilled with his car?"

"More than you can begin to know. He'd take it to bed with him, if I'd let him. You're his hero."

His hands tightened on the steering wheel. "Somebody should be, and your ex obviously doesn't want the job."

"Just as well. He's hardly the kind of role model I want for my son."

"I still wonder why fatherhood wasn't enough to keep the guy on the straight and narrow."

"I hoped it would, but the novelty of having a son soon wore off and he became worse than ever. It was as if he saw the baby as a daily reminder of his personal failure to father a child of his own. He began finding excuses to work late every night, then started disappearing for days at a stretch."

"Sounds like a real hands-on kind of dad, all right!"

"It was the old pattern repeating itself. When he did finally come home, his behavior was so unpredictable, I never knew what to expect. The awful thing was, Jeremy picked up on the tension and cried the whole time his father was around, which just made matters worse. Todd was resentful, I was exhausted and at my wit's end with worry, and my poor baby was miserable."

"Small wonder!" Michael let out an exclamation of disgust and took a corner so sharply, the tires squealed in protest. Alarmed, Camille braced her hand against the dashboard.

Realizing he'd frightened her, he eased his foot off the accelerator and said calmly, "Relax, Camille. I haven't killed a dinner date yet. I'll get us there and back in one piece, I promise.''

"I'm sure you will, but there's no great hurry, you know. We're making very good time.''

"I realize that. I just got so riled up with what you were telling me, I let my attention wander. Not a good idea, I know, especially in unfamiliar territory, but it won't happen again.''

He inhaled deeply and pointedly changed the subject. "Pretty countryside,'' he said, surveying the passing scenery. "Too bad it's getting dark already. I wouldn't mind coming back during the day and seeing more of it.''

"I'll be happy to act as tour guide, if you do.''

A second of silence spun by before he said, "Unfortunately, I doubt I'll have the time.''

What shocked her the most about his answer was not the reminder that he wouldn't be around much longer, but that the news should leave her so utterly desolate.

What was the matter with her? She'd always known he'd go, sooner or later. She'd encouraged their relationship precisely *because* she knew it would be short term: a fling, a brief encounter, no strings attached—and any number of other tired clichés on which she'd hung her decision to become involved with him.

But hearing him give voice to the inevitable cut through her smug delusions and laid bare the truth hidden underneath. *She did not want to lose him, not now, not ever!*

"I see,'' she said, dismay casting such a long shadow over the evening that she didn't know how she'd survive it. "You'll be leaving shortly, then?''

She had to ask. Not knowing—living with the fear that she'd wake up one morning and discover the reason she hadn't heard from him in days was that he'd left without saying goodbye—was more than she could face.

"I'll be leaving, yes. How soon I really can't say. I have a few…loose ends to tie up before I go and no idea how long that will take." His gaze lingered on her intently a moment before swinging back to the road, and although his words had been neutral enough, she thought she saw longing in his eyes, and a strange ambivalence.

It was all the encouragement needed for a tidal wave of hope to rush through her. Those loose ends he was referring to meant him and her. She knew it as surely as she knew her own name. All his talk about friendship was a front, just as his offhand dismissal of what had happened the other night had been. If he really didn't care about her, he'd never have bothered to contact her again. He wasn't ready to admit his real feelings, that was all, because he was a man, and men were more cautious than women when it came to love.

Love, Camille? When did "love" enter the picture?

"Camille? Am I right?"

He was applying the brakes. Almost bringing the car to a stop. Pinning her in his gaze, his expression inquiring. Hedgerows on either side cloaked the quiet back road in darkness, made it a private, intimate place. Her heart fluttered up into her throat. "…Right?"

"We turn at this intersection?"

"Oh," she said faintly, pressing a hand to her chest as her heart fell back where it belonged. "Oh, yes, right…I mean, left. You turn left."

His soft, sexy laughter flowed over her. "I've known dinner dates to fall asleep on the way home, but you're the first to pass out on me before you've been fed. I must be losing my touch."

Not you, Michael! You couldn't if you tried. "I wasn't sleeping," she said. "Just daydreaming."

Not long after, they reached the lodge, as famous for its

chateau style of architecture and acres of gardens as it was for its food. He'd secured a table in a quiet corner next to a window on the lower, fireplace level of the dining room.

"I'm glad I found out about this place," he said, once the wine-tasting ritual was out of the way and their oyster Rockefeller appetizer had been served. "I wanted to bring you someplace special tonight, and I'd say this fills the bill."

A man didn't bring a woman to a special place to give her the brush-off. He didn't need sterling and bone china and crystal set on table linen starched to a fare-thee-well to prove he was her friend. He didn't order champagne to toast the end of an affair. Steeling herself not to read too much into his every word and gesture, she said, "It is lovely, isn't it?"

He fixed her in another sober, heart-melting stare. "Not quite as lovely as you, Camille. The way you look tonight is something I'll remember long after I leave here."

As quickly as her hopes had soared, they sank again. Premonition, cool as midnight in February, stole over her. "I don't want to talk about your leaving," she said, shivering. "I want to learn more about *you*—about the kind of life you've lived. Who are you, Michael, when you're not playing tourist? What kind of hopes and dreams shaped you into the man you are today? Where do you see yourself, a year from now, and if you could have just one wish, what would it be?"

It had taken him a full five days to come to grips with what he knew he must, in all conscience, do. Their relationship had run off the main track and was headed down a dangerous side road built on a shifting foundation of deceit. Regardless of the cost to him, he had to put a stop to it.

He'd see her one last time, tell her the truth, and that would be it.

Once he'd made up his mind, he promised himself two things: he wouldn't lay a hand on her, no matter what the provocation, and he wouldn't let *anything* get in the way of his coming clean.

The first was easy. There'd be no dancing, no getting cozy beside a roaring fire, no playing footsies under the table, and definitely no fooling around in the car on the way back or accepting an invitation to come in for a nightcap.

The second he'd known would be difficult. He could hardly blurt out of the blue, "By the way, I've been meaning to tell you I'm your son's natural father."

But her spate of questions had handed him the perfect lead-in. All he had to do was answer her, and the truth would come out. Only a fool would turn away from such a heaven-sent chance to make a clean breast of everything.

He was a fool! Raising his glass in a silent toast, he said, "Not until you finish telling me your story."

She gave a little shrug, just enough to draw his eye to the low-cut front of her dress and the lovely honey-gold skin it revealed. "There's nothing else to tell."

"Sure there is," he said, gulping down a healthy swig of the champagne. He should have ordered something with more bite—something raw and bitter that would burn down a man's throat and bolster his courage—instead of a wine synonymous with the prelude to seduction. "When did you reach the end of your rope with Todd? Was it something specific or just battle fatigue in general?"

She shrugged again. *Damn!* "A bit of both, I suppose. His behavior was destroying him and everyone around him, and he didn't care enough to want to change. Perhaps if it had still been just the two of us, I might have tried harder to keep the marriage alive, but clearly it was no kind of environment for a child, so I took Jeremy and moved out and filed for divorce.''

''You mean, the place you're living in now isn't the one—?''

She shuddered, which was almost as distracting as if she'd shrugged. The top of her dress, what little there was of it, slithered over her breasts like a jealous lover. ''No! I wanted a completely fresh start, away from all the bad memories.''

Even though he cleared his throat, he still sounded like a choirboy in the midst of exchanging his soprano for a tenor. ''And he didn't fight you on it?''

''He was glad to see the back of us.''

Gad, Mike D'Alessandro wasn't the only fool walking around! ''The man must be a moron. Couldn't he see what he was giving up?''

She leaned forward so that even more of her cleavage showed. ''He had other priorities, Michael. People with addictive personalities are driven in ways you and I can't begin to understand. All that matters to them is catering to their obsession—whether it be power or money or mountain climbing. In Todd's case, it happened to be alcohol and eventually cocaine.''

''I can understand being driven,'' he said, forcing himself to concentrate on what she was saying, instead of what she was almost wearing. ''We've all got things—people, principles—that matter to us enough that we'll do just about anything to honor them. But I can't imagine anyone being willing to sacrifice a child.''

What the hell was he saying? Hadn't Kay jettisoned their marriage and their son because dancing in a chorus line and playing bit parts in a third rate Hollywood movie had mattered more?

"But that's how addicts are," Camille said earnestly. "They can't help themselves. Half the time, I don't think Todd was even aware of the effects his actions had on me or the baby."

"Uh-huh." He ran his finger inside the collar of his shirt and unbuttoned his jacket. Anything to take his mind off what he wanted, which was to touch her. She was so fine, so elegant.

"You're staring," she said, a smile lurking at the corners of her mouth. "Do I have spinach caught in my teeth?"

Awareness caught him off guard, triggering a soft implosion that almost had him groaning aloud. He shouldn't be looking at her; shouldn't be admiring her smooth complexion, the scalloped curve of her upper lip, the dimple in her chin.

Hers were not the features he should be committing to memory. He hadn't assumed a false identity and all the lies which went with it to make an ass of himself over a woman who, once she knew his true history, would plant her dainty foot in the seat of his pants and boot him out the door.

He'd done it for the too brief pleasure of sharing a few stolen days of his son's life. *Those* were the memories he should be hoarding against a future which of late had lost so much luster that he could barely bring himself to think about it.

"Let's order our main course," he said, grabbing the leather-bound menu and disappearing behind it before he did or said something really asinine. "You've been here before. What do you recommend?"

"The rack of lamb, the crab cakes.... Is something wrong, Michael? You seem upset."

"Yes, something's wrong!" he practically barked, slapping the menu closed. "The man you married made your life a living hell, not to mention your child's, yet you keep defending him.''

"I'm not defending him,'' she said, her eyes wide with dismay.

"You sure aren't condemning him!''

"I divorced him, Michael. What else should I have done, hired a hit man and had him shot?''

"Sounds like a pretty good idea to me.''

Before he realized what she intended, she slid her hand across the table and folded her fingers around his. "He gave me my baby. I'll always be grateful to him for that.''

The remark cut him to the quick. *Wrong, sweetheart!* he wanted to bellow. *I'm the one who did the giving!* Instead, he marshaled his vanishing control and avenged himself the only way he knew how. "Exactly how did he do that, Camille?''

She pulled her hand away and stared at him, surprised, he suspected, as much by the bitterness in his tone as by a question whose answer should have been evident to a congenital idiot. "How do you think, Michael?''

"Well, let's see.'' He leaned back in his chair and counted off his reply on his fingers. "One, he went to a registered adoption agency. Two, you were both subjected to several interviews with medical and psychological experts who put you under intense scrutiny to make sure you'd measure up as parents. Three, having passed all those tests with flying colors, you appeared before a judge or some other legal bigwig who approved your taking a baby, subject to a six month probationary period during which time a social worker dropped by without warning to see how things were going. How am I doing so far?''

She couldn't look at him. She glanced down at her hands, clasped tightly in her lap. Her lashes, their shadow stretched to ridiculous length by the candlelight, flared across the high arc of her cheekbones. Her mouth trembled. And he, damned fool that he was, wanted nothing so much as to take her in his arms and apologize for haranguing her.

If only she were just some woman he'd met socially…!

He left the thought unfinished, ticked off to discover that his body was already ten steps ahead of his brain. Just as well the waiter loomed up out of nowhere, somber as a black-clad angel, his head bald as a billiard ball decked out in a halo of white fluff. "Are you ready to order, sir?"

Michael shot an inquiring glance at Camille. She seemed on the verge of tears. "We'll both have the filet mignon," he decided, latching onto the first thing that came into his head. "Medium rare. And a bottle of your best Shiraz."

"Very good, sir." The waiter disappeared, leaving behind a cloud of silence, thick as the air before a thunderstorm.

Realizing he was drumming furiously on the table with the pads of his fingers, Michael clenched his fist and said, "Steak okay with you, Camille?"

She shook her head.

"You want me to cancel and order something else?"

She cast about the room, looking for all the world like a trapped doe. Finding no help on the inside, she fastened her gaze on the floodlit gardens outside. "Why are you doing this, Michael?"

"Doing what?"

He knew exactly what. And the pitying look she leveled at him told him *she* knew he was just playing for time. "Why are you cross-examining me as if I've committed a crime? Why do you care how we came to adopt Jeremy?"

"Maybe because I care about you."

"I'd like to think so, but the way you're acting…."

"I just find it strange that Todd's problems didn't raise a red flag with whoever looked into your family background. I don't pretend to be an expert on adoption rulings in California, but I know that in Canada, pretty stringent guidelines are laid down to protect children from the kind of home situation Jeremy fell into.''

She stroked her thumb over her pale pink nail polish. Twisted the pearl ring on the third finger of her right hand. And said in a voice so hushed he had to strain to hear it, ''Nobody interviewed us. Todd heard through a colleague that there was a woman in Los Angeles desperate to find a home for her unborn child. We went to meet her, and the three of us worked out an arrangement.''

''Worked out an arrangement?''

''There was nothing fishy about it, if that's what you're implying,'' she said sharply. ''We undertook to pay her medical expenses and help her make a fresh start after the birth, and she agreed to let us take her baby. Todd drew up the necessary documents and the three of us signed them with two of his law firm partners acting as witnesses. You already know all this, Michael, so I don't know why you're bringing the subject up again.''

''Yes. And I still have a hard time believing it never occurred to you that there should have been more to it than that.''

''Why should it have, when everything was perfectly in order?''

He threw up his hands in disbelief. ''Because from what you've told me, it's plain that the only thing you signed was an agreement for sale. You bought a black market baby, Camille.''

A delicate flush rode over her face. ''That's absurd! I did no such thing. And what gives you the right to sit in judgment of my actions, anyway? Just who do you think you are?''

Oh, sweetheart, if you only knew! But he couldn't tell

her now. He'd put her on the defensive and there was no way he'd get her to receive the truth kindly at this point. Furthermore, he was too steamed to try.

Biting down on the urge to pound his fist on the table and bellow, *That commodity you bought happened to be my son and I'd have seen you all in hell before I'd have let you have him, if I'd known,* he mustered the dregs of his composure and said, "I'm trying to be your friend, Camille."

"I fail to see how."

"Then that makes us equal, because I fail to understand how a woman as educated and sophisticated as you appear to be can take at face value everything that's handed to her."

"Maybe because I'm too trusting and a little bit naive."

"You adopt a baby knowing your husband's a lush and your marriage is on the skids. You swallow wholesale his story of just happening to find a pregnant woman living in a flea-pit motel in L.A. and—"

"How did you know he found her in a motel? I never told you that."

"If she'd been living in luxury, she wouldn't have needed rescuing," he said, breaking out in a fine sweat. Many more slips like that, and he wouldn't have to admit a thing. She'd figure the whole story out for herself. "It could have been a mansion, for all I care. The point I'm making is, he comes up with a woman conveniently waiting for a couple with money to pick her up, clean her off, pay her bills and buy her baby for a princely sum. And you don't raise a peep of protest when neither a judge nor a social worker is involved in the arrangement. You never once ask to see *both* parents' consent to the adoption." He shook his head in disgust. "I don't call that trusting and naive, Camille, I call it stupid. And perhaps a little too self-serving. I think you used an innocent baby to try to shore up your sinking marriage.''

Her eyes gleamed with unshed tears, but they stemmed as much from anger as hurt. Spots of color burned on her cheeks. Her breasts rose and fell in agitation. ''I did nothing of the sort,'' she said, the pulse at her throat racing so hard he could see it. ''I thought my marriage was back on track. And we didn't just go shopping one day and come home with a baby, you know! We spent the last four months of the pregnancy with the birth mother, in part to give her the chance to be sure adoption was the route she wanted to take, but mostly to prepare ourselves to become parents.''

''And a fat lot of good it did you! The so-called father takes off within weeks of the kid's birth, leaving you to do double duty as a single parent. Not what you'd call an *ideal* arrangement, is it?''

The hurt won out over the anger. ''Don't you think I already know that?'' she cried softly, the tears rolling down her face. ''Don't you think I lie awake at nights, worrying about how much my son's missing by not having a father around—of how much he's been cheated? Of course I do! Maybe I'm every bit the fool you say I am, Michael, but I love my son with my whole heart and I'd give anything— *anything!*—not to have had things turn out the way they did. But I don't know what you expect me to do about it at this late stage. I might have bought a baby, according to the way you see things, but I'll be damned if I'm going to run out and buy a husband, just to fulfill your idea of what a family's all about!''

''Oh, jeez, Camille!'' He shoved his napkin at her. ''Here, dry your eyes. So help me, I didn't bring you here to ream you out and make you miserable. It's just that every time I think about your scheming bastard of an ex-husband,

I see red. It's not just Jeremy who deserved better. You did, too.''

She opened her mouth to reply, and let out a sob instead that had half the diners in the room looking their way.

He clapped a hand to his forehead. The way things were going, he'd have a lynch mob after his hide before long. ''Please, Camille, stop crying.''

To her credit, she tried. She bit her lip until he thought it would bleed. She swallowed as painfully as if she'd got an orange stuck in her throat. She turned to stare out of the window so that he couldn't see her face. But the tears kept coming, sparkling from the ends of her lashes and splashing onto the fancy beadwork on her dress.

The waiter reappeared. ''Your wine, sir,'' he began, then stopped with the bottle poised in midair. Concern furrowed his brow and sent wrinkles chasing up his shiny dome of a head as Camille pressed her napkin to her mouth and pushed away from the table. Strangling on another sob, she made a dash for the open door to the patio.

''We've changed our minds. Maybe later....'' Already on his feet, Michael waved the waiter aside and went after her.

By the time he got outside, she'd vanished. There was no sign of her on the steps leading to the gardens, but unless she'd vaulted over the lush flower beds on either side, which seemed unlikely given the cut of her dress, she had to have taken the path winding under trees strung with little white lights.

She had, but even so he might easily have missed her if it hadn't been for her muffled sobs leading him to where she huddled on a bench in a secluded alcove formed by a ten-foot-high hedge with a keyhole entrance carved in it.

Figuring he'd screwed up enough to invalidate his hands-off promise, he dropped next to her on the bench and took her in his arms. Just to comfort her. Just so that he could stroke her back until her shoulders stopped heaving and she was feeling better.

Then he'd confess.

And tell her she had nothing to fear from him because all he wanted was to see his son occasionally and contribute to his life however she'd let him.

And hope she'd believe him and feel inclined to be generous.

CHAPTER SEVEN

SHE huddled in his arms, her heart going a mile a minute like a terrified, injured bird's. And it was all his fault. What the devil was wrong with him? Was he really so unsure of his own claims that he had to trample all over hers before he found the guts to come out with the truth?

Tucking her head beneath his chin, he pressed his hand to the side of her face. Her tears scalded his fingers, but it was her hopeless efforts to get herself under control that damn near broke his heart.

"I'm not worth it, you know," he muttered against her hair. "If you're going to make yourself sick crying over somebody, it shouldn't be for some fool shooting his mouth off on matters he knows nothing about."

Another partial lie, but necessary under the circumstances. Jeremy was his son, regardless of who'd been named father on the birth certificate, but if he was looking to point the finger of blame at someone for the omission, that person was Kay. *She* was the one who'd robbed him of his rights, and he had no business trying to shift responsibility for his loss to the woman whose only sin had been that she wanted his baby a lot more than Kay ever had.

So tell her that, you dumb schmuck! Quit procrastinating and lay it all out for her.

Before he could begin though, Camille drew in a breath that left her slender frame shaking like a leaf caught in the wind, and said in a waterlogged voice, "I knew."

"Knew what, love?" he asked cautiously.

But she'd slipped into a private inner world where he

couldn't follow, and seemed not to hear him. Sitting up a little straighter, she pushed her hair back from her face and stared blindly at the tall hedge surrounding them. "I asked him, and he told me not to interfere. He said it was his job to take care of the legal end of things, and mine to learn to change a diaper. But I knew...it was all too sudden, too easy. I *knew* something wasn't right. I've always known. And it terrifies me."

"Unless you deliberately falsified the facts in order to cheat the mother out of her child, you have no reason to worry," he said, finally cluing in to what she was going on about. "She isn't going to show up at your door and demand her child back."

That much, at least, was the absolute truth.

"But *he* could."

"Todd?" He stroked his knuckles down her cheek to her jaw. "Honey, you said yourself—"

"Not him," she said. "The other one. The *real* father."

"I guarantee he'll never make trouble for you."

Another truth, but pitifully inadequate when stacked up against the mountain of deceit still waiting to be exposed.

She turned her head and regarded him solemnly a moment, then a small dreamy smile flitted across her face. "You sound so sure, I almost believe you."

How many heaven-sent chances was he going to blow before he quit dancing around the subject? Even if she despised him for waiting so long to reveal the whole sad story, telling her would leave him with the satisfaction of knowing he'd put her fears to rest for good.

"Look," he said, bracing himself for her reaction, "a little while ago, you said you wanted to know all about me—about who I really am."

"I've changed my mind." She swivelled in his lap, the better to look at him. The tears were done. Her eyes were big and luminous, and very beautiful. Her words whispered over his mouth, flavored with champagne. The tips of her breasts touched lightly against his shirtfront. When she moved, silky underthings rustled against her skin, and he remembered how she'd felt when he'd run his hands over her naked body.

"Huh?" he croaked, dizzy with the scent and sound and feel of her.

"I said, I've changed my mind."

"How come?"

"Because I already know everything that matters."

"You don't know beans." He touched his finger to her lips to silence her, and was caught completely unprepared when she drew the tip into her mouth. The aftershock flew straight as an arrow to his groin. *Bull's-eye!*

Things were not going according to plan. Not one little bit. He was fast losing his grip. Shoving good intentions aside, his mind was doing what it always seemed to do best whenever he found himself alone with her: taking up residence in his nether regions.

"I know you're honorable and decent and kind," she said, removing her finger and fixing her gaze on his mouth instead. How she managed to talk rationally when he could scarcely breathe stupefied him. "I know you've showered Jeremy with more attention than Todd ever did and certainly brought him more pleasure. That by itself is reason enough for me to be glad I met you."

"I think—"

"That I'm going a bit overboard with the compliments?" She gave another of those distracting little shrugs that left him squirming. "Don't worry, I'm not going to embarrass either of us by pretending we're anything more than the proverbial ships passing in the night. But that doesn't alter the fact that when I'm upset, you make me feel better. You call me sweetheart and honey as if you mean it, and it's been such a long time since anyone did that.''

"I—!"

"Let me finish, please, before I lose my nerve." She sketched a tender finger over his eyebrow. "You make me face my demons, something I was unable to do before I met you. Most of all, you're not afraid to tell me the truth."

"Stop it!" he ground out, closing his eyes to avoid having to witness the honesty in hers. "You don't know what the hell you're talking about."

"I know that you've been my friend and that means everything to me." She moved closer. Too close. Her breath tumbled over his face, fresh as a spring morning. "Thank you, Michael," she said softly, and kissed him on the cheek. Then, with another rustling of silk, she slithered off his lap.

How the touch of her lips—bestowed with a guileless sincerity that was almost childlike—could translate into a kiss so loaded with sexual promise that it electrified him, defied explanation.

Nor did he waste time trying to come up with one. "Where are you going?"

"Back to the dining room. I think I've said enough."

He tussled with his conscience, telling himself that if he could do nothing else right, in this instance at least he could live up to her lofty perceptions of him and let her go. To try to keep her there because he couldn't control the hunger raging through him, was indefensible.

"Stay…!" Ignoring his pitiful attempt at nobility, the word tore loose from his throat, half command, half plea.

She paused on the brink of flight, her head tilted in such a way that her profile shone pale and perfect against the dark foliage of the hedge. Helpless to prevent himself, he

curved his arm around her hips and turned her to face him
again.

Just one more little kiss, he promised himself, all the
time knowing that, where she was concerned, a little was
never enough.

Even so, scruples still might have won the day had that
damnable slit in her skirt not trapped his hand so that, as
she pivoted toward him, his palm slid beneath the fabric
and closed over her thigh.

If he'd had any sort of moral fiber, he'd have stopped
right there and then, instead of groping around blindly,
worse than a horny eighteen-year-old making out with a
high school cheerleader.

Trouble was, cheerleaders wore tight-fitting drawers and
panty hose to keep them decent while they flung themselves
around on the football field. But Camille had on silk stock-
ings which left three inches of bare skin at the top of her
thighs, and skimpy satin panties which offered no resistance
at all to his finger inching past the elasticized lace to caress
the fleecy-soft hair between her legs.

He was lost, and he knew it.

And so was she. She crumpled forward and if he hadn't
held her pinned between his knees, she'd have collapsed
on the gravel at his feet. Instead, she swayed toward him,
her head drooping on the slender stem of her neck like a
fading flower.

"Ah!" she exclaimed, on a fractured breath.

She was tight and moist and so ready for him that with
one touch to the sensitized bud hidden in the sweet folds
of her flesh, he brought her to orgasm—and came close to
it himself.

He wanted her naked beneath him, on a bed, with candlelight glimmering over her skin. He wanted to kiss every

inch of her; to put his mouth where his hand was and taste the honeydew sweetness of her release.

He wanted to remain buried inside her for long, deep minutes at a stretch, and watch her eyes glaze over and her mouth fall softly open just before she came. He wanted to move within her slowly and deliberately, surfing the waves of passion time and again until, at last, with his heart fit to burst, they hammered him into submission.

He could have done all that and more. The lodge offered overnight accommodation. For the price of a room and fifteen minutes of patience, he could have secluded her in privacy and comfort, and taken the rest of the night to pleasure her.

But she, still vibrating helplessly against him, fumbled to open his fly and reached inside to cup him in the palm of her hand. The agony increased a notch, raking through him and threatening imminent destruction.

Fifteen minutes?

The sweat sprang out on his forehead and prickled the length of his spine. The speed with which he was losing ground, he feared he had less than fifteen seconds in which to hike up her skirt and yank down her underwear. Smothering a groan, he skimmed her dainty panties down her legs.

He thought he heard the faint tearing of silk. He hoped not; hoped he hadn't damaged that gorgeous dress. But it was a secondary concern, overshadowed by the certain knowledge that unless he put an end to the exquisite torment she was inflicting, he'd spill into her hands long before he could enter her, and that would be the end of it.

With the slit of her skirt spread wide over her thighs, he cradled her hips and hauled her astride him. Felt the sweet, damp flesh between her parted legs settle snugly against him, and with one mighty thrust, plunged inside her as the perimeter of his control started to crumble.

She closed around him, tight and sleek. Gritting his teeth, he fought to hang on just long enough to reawaken the faint echoes of pleasure still rippling through her frame. The bench was narrow, hard, unaccommodating. Whether by instinct or design, she drew her knees up and hooked her heels behind his waist in a frantic attempt to weld herself more seamlessly against him.

Supporting her with both hands, he tilted his hips up, driving ever deeper in a fruitless attempt to lose all of himself inside her. The move destroyed him. As the distant thunder of release gained strength, relentlessly drowning out everything but the frantic beat of her heart against his, he buried his mouth at her ear and started to tell her he was sorry.

But it was too late. The dam burst and ripped through him, trapping the words in his throat and pummeling him without mercy. Caught in its fury, she clung to him, her fists clenching reflexively at his shoulders, her eyes flying wide in a sightless stare. Painful, staccato breaths puffed from between her parted lips, as if her lungs were squeezing the very life out of her.

For a long moment, she hung suspended on the edge of sanity. He felt the heated flush ride over her, the quiver that ruffled her skin. And then, with a series of inarticulate little cries, she contracted around him, racked by spasm after spasm of splendid anguish.

Crushing her to him, he rode the dying swells to a perfect calm. He had never felt more connected to another, never more complete.

Paradise, though, was short-lived. Too soon, the real world swam back into focus and he had to face what he'd done. Unable to look at her, he eased her off his lap.

She teetered unsteadily a moment, like a sleepwalker rudely awakened. Her hair lay tousled around her face, and her dress was rucked around her hips.

Ashamed at the destruction he'd wrought, he went to ease the skirt into place. As he did so, something pale and flimsy near her right shoe caught his attention and he saw that her panties were hooked around her right ankle like a flag proclaiming his unconscionable behavior.

Stooping, he lifted her other foot and threaded it through the appropriate opening, but stopped short of pulling the garment up her legs. "I think you'd better take care of the rest," he muttered, and turned away to fumble with his own state of undress while she put herself to rights.

Except, there was no putting right what he'd done. He'd let self-indulgence displace caution, not to mention common decency, and treated her with an appalling lack of dignity and respect. Why she didn't haul off and sock him in the jaw he didn't know.

"I shouldn't have let that happen," he finally mumbled, still too ashamed to look her in the eye. "It's a bit late to express regret, I know, but when I'm with you...."

He trailed off, painfully aware of how lame he sounded.

"Don't be sorry, Michael," she said. "I'm not."

"How can you be so forgiving? For Pete's sake, I put my needs first, without any regard for yours."

"You're wrong. You made me feel beautiful and desirable."

"You are desirable, Camille, that's the problem and if, in his more lucid moments, your ex-husband forgot to mention that, he's got one more to add to his list of sins." He shook his head in self-disgust, and started toward the keyhole opening in the hedge. "I don't know about you, but I've lost my appetite for food. I think it's best if I just take you home."

"Walking away isn't going to change anything, you know," she said.

He stopped and swung back to face her, guilt making him surly. "If that's supposed to mean something profound, you've lost me."

"You're afraid, Michael."

"Huh?"

"You're afraid to face your real feelings. You're hoping I'll tell you never to come near me again, then you won't have to deal with what really happened tonight."

"I know exactly what happened tonight, I assure you," he said grimly. "I took advantage of you when your defenses were down. In my book, that makes me lower than dirt."

"Are you at all interested in knowing how I feel?"

"Used?" he suggested, resorting to sarcasm to cover up the fact that he couldn't stand himself. "Abused?"

"Loved."

"Oh, jeez!" He thumped a fist to his forehead. "Don't go glamorizing what we did. Love has nothing to do with it."

"Then what does?" she said. "The way I see it, what we shared adds up to something a bit more momentous than having a bad hair day."

"We had sex."

"Oh, Michael, if you really believed all we'd done was have sex, your conscience wouldn't be bothering you now to the point that you can't wait to get rid of me. You'd play the perfect date, buy me a nice dinner, and consider the score even. No apologies, no remorse, and definitely no regrets."

"I like to think I'm not quite that crass," he said, wincing at the radiance of her smile.

"You're not. You're a very nice man who holds himself

accountable for his actions, and you know how to make a woman feel…good.'' She smoothed her hands down her dress one last time, combed her fingers through her hair, and came toward him. ''But that doesn't mean you owe me anything more than you're able to give, okay? I know you'll be leaving soon, and although I wish you didn't have to go, I'm not fool enough to think you're going to rear-range your life on the strength of a three-week relationship. I'm just saying I'm grateful for what we've had. It's been wonderful, Michael. I'll treasure the memories for the rest of my life. You'll be the summer fling I'll remember with fondness when I'm old and gray. End of story.''

It wasn't often that he was caught at a loss for words, and even rarer that he found himself so moved that his eyes burned with the threat of tears. Quite by accident, he'd come across a jewel of a woman, and like the undeserving boor he undoubtedly was, he'd not recognized her worth until it was too late. And thanks to his stalling tactics, it most certainly was too late.

To tell her now that he was her child's natural father, and expect her to accept that he hadn't deliberately wormed his way into her heart for the sole purpose of getting closer to his son was asking for a miracle he didn't deserve.

Burying a sigh, he left her in the car, went back to settle his bill at the lodge, then took her home. The drive was memorable in that they exchanged not a word the entire time. When they reached her house, he walked her as far as the flight of the steps outside her front door, and no further.

Realizing that as far as he was concerned, the evening was over, she turned to face him one last time. ''Well,'' she said, with an uncertain smile, ''I guess the only thing left to say is thank you for a lovely time and good night.''

He didn't reply. Instead, he gazed at her, committing to

memory her lovely heart-shaped face. He saw her smile fade, and her mouth tremble. He saw how she lowered her eyes so that he wouldn't see how filled with hurt they were. And he saw how she drew on the breeding and class that were her trademark to get herself inside and away from him before her pride collapsed.

Not until the door had closed behind her did he finally speak the only words left to say. "Goodbye, Camille."

Then he climbed back into his car and took off, knowing it all had to end here. If he wanted to retain a shred of self-respect, his only recourse was to leave her in ignorance, and if that meant he'd never see Jeremy again then he had only himself to blame.

She had given so much, and all he'd ever done was take. He couldn't hurt her more than he already had, and he couldn't go on punishing himself, either.

He'd found a son. He'd briefly known the joy of being a father, albeit in secret. But for everyone's sake, he had to leave it at that and walk away before he caused everyone more pain.

She would not cry. She would remember instead how he had loved her—how his kisses had swept aside her inhibitions, how the flush of passion had swept over her body and she'd let it take her where it would. And she would trust the instincts which told her that it wasn't over between them. She'd hold on to the conviction that his feelings for her ran deeper than he was willing to admit and that he'd realize it, once he'd dealt with his guilt. She would not give up on him until he made a clean and final break with her.

It was the only way she could get through the night.

Morning, though, cast the truth in a much harsher light and revealed her instincts for the wishful thinking they really were. She might have been foolish enough to fall in love, but Michael was made of sterner stuff. His life did not coincide with hers, and if she'd been in any doubt about that, her parents, showing up uninvited just after lunch, certainly brought the message home in a way she couldn't ignore.

"I don't imagine you're going to like what you're about to hear, but that can't be helped," her father began. "As you're well aware, your mother and I have been disturbed—deeply disturbed—by your apparent infatuation with Michael D'Alessandro. Camille, you have to put an end to this association. The man is not to be trusted."

"How do you know that?"

"Because I had him investigated."

She stared at her father in scandalized disbelief. "You did *what?*"

"I hired someone to look into his background. I felt I had no choice."

"No *choice?* Dad, you had no *right!*"

"You're my daughter and that gives me the right. Having to watch the hell Todd put you through and knowing I was helpless to do anything about it was bad enough. If you think I'm going to stand idly by and let it happen a second time, you greatly underestimate the power of a father's love, Camille."

"Michael is as different from Todd as night is from day."

"In one respect he certainly is," her mother put in. "Whatever Todd's faults, he always managed to look after his investments. He never let anything, not even his…ahem, little problem, interfere with his work. The same can hardly be said of your latest admirer. Less than two years ago, a series of bad business decisions left Michael D'Alessandro on the brink of financial ruin."

"Are you saying he's bankrupt, Mother? Is that what you

were trying to tell me the other day, when you warned me the only reason he could possibly be interested in me is for my money?''

''What we're telling you,'' her father said flatly, ''is that although he's made a remarkable comeback, he's in no position to be frittering away his time on your doorstep because he's in the mood for a month of fun in the sun. He has business obligations in Vancouver requiring his attention—matters the foreman he left in charge is not qualified to handle, which begs the question why, just when he's poised for considerable success on his own turf, he's setting up camp at your front door.''

''Maybe because I've made it clear he's welcome here.''

''I'm afraid, my dear, we've uncovered another reason which has nothing at all to do with you.''

Until then, her parents' suspicions had struck her as preposterous, largely because nothing they had said countered what she already knew. But her father's smug certainty that he'd found a rattlesnake in her bed and that she was too stupid to recognize its danger roused her to a rash, defensive anger. ''Before either of you says another word, you should be aware that I'm in love with Michael and if he were to ask me to move to Canada to be with him, I'd be gone in a shot. *That's* how much I believe in him.''

Her mother let out a yelp and pressed a hand to her heart. ''You cannot be serious, Camille!''

But her father merely sighed and said grimly, ''I was hoping matters hadn't progressed quite that far. I hoped you would show more sense than to throw in your lot with a stranger. Dare I ask if he returns your feelings?''

To tell them the truth was more than she could bear, but lying was not an option either, so she struck a middle ground. ''I haven't asked him.''

Her father removed a slip of paper from his pocket. ''Before you do, my dear, you might want to do a little investigating of your own based on this.''

Glad that he couldn't see how her heart had started to race, she took the paper and read the information printed on it. *Room 4, 7 West, St. Mary's Hospital, San Francisco.*

''Is this supposed to mean something to me?''

''It will, once you discover who it is he's been spending most of his time with. I think it will prove conclusively that he's been lying to you from the minute he walked into your life.''

The morning after the dinner fiasco, he drove into San Francisco and checked into a small hotel near the hospital. Kay's time had dwindled to a matter of days, if not hours, and it made more sense to be close by. Or so he told himself, and that was the story he was sticking to, because to acknowledge the other reason—that he was voluntarily walking out of Jeremy's life without so much as a goodbye—was just too damned painful to deal with.

Kay seemed brighter when he visited her that afternoon. ''I didn't think you'd come until later,'' she said, reaching for his hand.

''I wanted to be sure I caught you before you went to sleep. I've got something to show you.''

He'd been carrying the photos with him for days, but he'd held out showing them to her for fear that seeing them would upset her too much. But the clock was winding down and he didn't have to be a doctor to know it. Pretty soon, she'd be past caring.

He cranked up the bed a little and spread the pictures on the fold of the sheet in front of her. ''This is our boy, Kay. What do you think of him?''

Her eyes, already huge in her sunken face, glowed like coals, but it was the smile transforming her face that choked him. "Oh, my baby!" she whispered, running her fingers over the face of the child she'd given away. "Oh, my precious little angel! Look at him, Mike. He reminds me of you."

"Nah," he said, doing his damnedest not to lose it. "He's the living image of you when I first met you. Remember that day?"

"You were playing basketball at U.B.C."

"And you were the cheerleader whose lap I landed in when I tried to keep the ball in play."

"You said I had great legs."

Oh, honey, he thought, squeezing his eyes shut against the pain of seeing the way she looked now. *You had great everything in those days.*

"I wish we'd been able to make it work, Mike."

He cleared his throat and stroked her arm. No use pointing out that he'd tried. No use, either, pointing out that she'd had her sights set on a career in show business, and there'd been no talking her out of it.

To be fair though, he hadn't put up much resistance when she'd said she wanted a divorce. They'd been college sweethearts who'd married more because they were used to each other than anything else. Once the bloom wore off, they'd shared little more than a bed. The way he'd seen it, when the only thing a man and woman had in common was good sex, there wasn't much hope the relationship was going to last over the long haul, and even the sex hadn't been all that good toward the end.

She thrashed her head from side to side like a trapped animal desperately seeking escape and finding none. Her lips were cracked and dry, her color the ghastly yellow of fading bruises. "I sold my soul to the devil...traded my baby for fame and glamor."

"Hush," he murmured, wiping her face with a damp

cloth. "You made a mistake, honey, but it's time to forgive yourself."

"I was good, you know…the lead dancer in a nightclub, Mike…my name up in lights. Rita Osborne…just like the devil promised…." The rambling drifted into exhaustion and her eyes closed.

Michael believed in God. Growing up in the heart of Vancouver's Italian community, he hadn't known a kid who didn't. Church on Sunday, being an altar boy, singing in the choir—they were as much a part of life as home-made pasta. But it had been years since he'd prayed.

He prayed then, though, because it was all there was left that he could do. *Take her home,* he begged, his eyes misting over as he watched each labored breath leach a little more strength out of her. *She's paid enough.*

She stirred. Plucked restlessly at the sheet. "He said he'd make me a star, you know."

"Who, the devil?"

"No, silly," she said, all at once sounding completely lucid. "My agent. But he didn't. He just took all my money. And when I told him I was pregnant, he told me no one would hire a woman sticking out a mile in front to dance in a chorus line."

So that was why she'd been destitute when Todd Whitfield had found her! Some scam artist had robbed her blind. "Money doesn't really matter much in the overall scheme of things, Kay," he said.

"It does when it's time to pay. A pound of flesh, Mike, right?" Her face contorted into a hideous rictus of amusement. "Except a pound wasn't enough, was it?" Her hands fluttered weakly over her wasted body. "There's nothing left of me."

"Kay…!" *Oh, God, please help her. Help me!*

"When they told me I was going to die, I had to come

back…had to find my baby and see…for myself. But I left it too late…."

"The devil's had his due, Kay," he said. "You're paid up in full. Our boy's in good hands. Loving hands. You can rest easy now."

"Yes," she said on a whisper, her eyes drifting shut once more. "Yes."

For a while longer, he sat with her, watching the slow, steady throb of the pulse in her throat. Wishing it would stop. Afraid that it might.

What a hell of a way for a thirty-five-year-old woman to die—in a ten-by-ten foot hospital room, and no one who gave a damn that she was alone in the world except an ex-husband. No friends to give comfort, no phone calls, no cards to pin to the corkboard above the bed, and the only flowers those he brought in every couple of days. Stargazer lilies, her favorite—but even their exotic scent couldn't overpower the smell of death that clung to her.

The door swished open to admit one of the nurses who regularly looked after Kay. "Why don't you take a break, Mr. D'Alessandro?" she said. "Go get yourself something to eat. Take a walk outside and get some fresh air. It'll do you a world of good."

"I hate to leave her alone."

"She won't be alone. I'll sit with your wife until you come back and if there's any change, I'll have you paged."

"Thanks." He needed to get away for a while and clear his head. He had the feeling it was going to be a very long night. "I'll turn on my phone if I leave the building. They've got my number at the nurses' station."

He was almost at the door when Kay stirred. "Mike?"

"I'm here," he said.

"I love you, Mike."

He paused on the threshold, briefly at a loss. How was he supposed to respond?

The answer came, clean and simple. Whatever she'd done or not done, she didn't deserve to die believing no one cared. She'd been his wife at one time; she'd borne his son. They were reasons enough to keep a special place in his heart just for her. So he told her the only truth that mattered anymore.

"I love you, too, honey."

CHAPTER EIGHT

HE WAS wiping his eyes as he came out into the corridor, and didn't see her lurking a few yards away. Numbly, Camille watched as he turned the corner to the elevators.

Part of her wanted to run after him, and comfort him. He didn't strike her as a man easily given to tears and her heart broke a little at the sadness draped over him like a shroud. But another part of her wanted to shriek in anguish because, without meaning to, she'd overheard too much.

I hate to leave her alone....

I'll sit with your wife....

I love you, too, honey....

He'd told her he was divorced, and she'd believed him. He'd told her the reason he went to the city was that he had business there, and she'd believed that, as well.

He'd come from his sick wife's bedside and within the hour made love to *her*. She'd rolled around without a stitch of clothing on, in the sand down by the river, and let him touch her all over. *Let him have sex.*

She'd listened to him lecture her about adopting a baby when her marriage was on the skids, and been grateful when he'd forgiven her enough to seduce her a second time.

She'd as good as told her parents never to darken her doorstep again, unless they were prepared to take back all the horrible things they'd said about him. She'd invited him into her home, introduced him to her son.

She'd let him make a fool of her, over and over again, and if she had a grain of sense, she'd go home to Jeremy and forget she'd ever met a man called Michael

D'Alessandro. She was obviously much better suited to being a mother than she was a lover.

But, like an open wound begging for attention, curiosity pulled at her, drawing her toward the window in the door through which he'd just left. What was she like, that woman on the other side whose adulterous husband had betrayed her all the time he was telling her he loved her? Why was she in a San Francisco hospital? They had hospitals up there in Canada, didn't they? And doctors?

Camille stole closer, intending to sneak a look through the pane of glass when suddenly the door swung open and a nurse came out carrying a water carafe. "I'll be back in a couple of minutes, but it's okay if you want to go in for a visit while I'm gone," she said, hurrying past. "She's sleeping a lot now, but talk to her anyway. Let her know you're there. We think it helps."

She ought not to go in. It wasn't any of her business. But though her conscience told her that, Camille's feet had a mind of their own and dragged her inexorably over the threshold and into the room.

She was aware of nothing but the scent of lilies in the air, and the figure lying so motionless on the bed that, for one horrified moment, she thought the woman was dead. Was backing stealthily toward the door, in fact, when the body gave a spasmodic twitch and gasped, "Mike?"

Camille froze, torn between pity and an irrational terror which urged her to flee the scene. But the woman—Mrs. D'Alessandro—seemed so distressed that in the end, pity won the day. Approaching the foot of the bed, Camille said, "He stepped out for a minute. Is there something I can do for you?"

"Thirsty," the poor thing managed, rolling her head from side to side.

A tumbler of chipped ice stood on a nearby table.

Dropping her bag on a chair, Camille took a tissue from the box by the sink and tipped several slivers of ice into it. "Here," she said, turning the poor, ravaged face toward her so that she could slip the melting ice between the dry, colorless lips. "This will help."

Her eyes were closed. The skin was drawn so tautly over her features that they'd shrunk to the size of a child's. But she'd been a beauty in her day, the high cheekbones and delicate jaw attested to that, and she'd been a redhead although little was left of her hair.

She was without question a stranger, her body wasted by disease almost to nothing, yet looking at her, Camille was haunted by a sense of familiarity. "Who is it that you remind me of?" she said softly, more to prod her own memory than because she expected a reply.

But as if she were trying to answer, his wife spoke again, an incoherent muttering this time, and picked weakly at the bedcovers as though searching for something—a slight movement only, but enough to dislodge what appeared to be colorful postcards hidden by a fold in the sheet. They slid between the guard rails and landed facedown on the floor under the chair.

Realizing she'd lost them, she groped for a handhold and tried to sit up, but the effort exhausted her. "My baby!" she cried on a thin wail of distress, sinking back against the pillows.

Camille's heart swelled with fresh pity. Oh, how frail and thin she was, how transparent her skin! "Please, Mrs. D'Alessandro, don't upset yourself," she begged, scooting down and reaching under the chair. "Your postcards are right here. I'll get them for you."

But they weren't postcards at all. They were photographs. Of Jeremy gleefully kicking a football on the lawn in front of her house. Of Jeremy, all dark tousled hair and big brown eyes, posing proudly beside his new red roadster.

"*What on earth…?*" Hands shaking, Camille picked up the snapshots, telling herself there was a logical explanation for finding them in that stark little hospital room. But the reasons tumbling through her mind made no sense. Why would a man bring pictures of another woman's child to his dying wife's bedside, and why would that poor soul think they were of her baby—unless…?

Time slowed, lumbered back nearly four years, and froze in horrifying detail to the last time Camille had been in a hospital.

December the eleventh, two days after Jeremy was born. She'd dressed him in a pale blue terry-cloth sleeper and a white hooded jacket she'd knitted herself. He'd looked adorable.

"*We'll take good care of him,*" *she'd promised his pretty auburn-haired birth mother.*

"*I know you will,*" *Rita Osborne had said, tucking the envelope Todd have given her into her purse. "He'll have a much better life with you.*"·

Stricken, Camille stared at the photographs and flinched at the clammy dread of certainty closing over her.

"Please…!" Full of yearning and heartbreak, the entreaty floated on a wilting breath from the high bed.

As slowly as if she were a hundred years old, Camille clutched the arm of the chair and pried herself upright. Michael D'Alessandro's dying wife was watching her, her huge, dark eyes wide open and desperate. And Camille knew then what it was that made the woman look so familiar when everything else about her had changed.

The face and body might be ravaged beyond recognition by illness, but the eyes—dear God, the eyes were a replica of Jeremy's. The resemblance was unmistakable. Indisputable.

"Rita?" she gasped, recognition flooding through her just before the floor swam up to meet her, and a world grown suddenly menacing faded into black.

She came to on a gurney in some sort of supply room lined with white cabinets. Her forehead throbbed and a nurse was taking her pulse. "Ugh!" she groaned, squinting against the bright overhead light. "What happened?"

"You fainted," the nurse said, swatting Camille's hand away when she reached up to investigate the weight on her forehead. "Don't mess with the icepack, sweetie. It's there to help reduce the swelling. You took quite a dive and smacked your head on the side of the bed. Good thing we heard the racket, or you'd still be lying on the floor."

"I never faint," she said, with feeble indignation.

"That's what they all say, until it hits home."

"It?" She wished the room would stop spinning. Wished someone would tell her how and why she was there to begin with.

The nurse stroked her cheek kindly. "Watching a loved one die takes a terrible toll on family and friends."

At that, everything came rushing back in ghastly detail, and for a moment Camille was afraid she might pass out again. But she couldn't afford the luxury. "I've got to get out of here," she said, struggling to sit up. "I need to be with my little boy."

"You're in no shape to be going anywhere just yet."

"You don't understand. I *have* to go to him." *Quickly, before Michael D'Alessandro beat her to it.*

"Not a chance, sweetie. Not until we contact someone to come and get you."

"I don't need anyone. I have my car here and can drive myself home."

"Uh-uh!" The nurse shook her head. "There's no way you're getting behind the wheel of a car in your condition. I'll bring in a phone and you can call your husband or a friend to come and pick you up. Hopefully, by the time he gets here, you'll be able to stand up under your own steam without keeling over. Meantime, stay put."

"You don't understand," Camille began again, but she was talking to an empty room. The nurse had bustled out, certain her word was law and no one would dare thwart it.

Much she knew! No one was going to keep Camille there against her will, not when Michael D'Alessandro was on the loose with criminal intent in mind! She might have hit her head when she fainted, but her brain still worked well enough for her to figure out what he was after.

He wanted Jeremy. Her son—*his* son!—was all he'd *ever* wanted, and all the rest—the compliments, the kisses, the sex—had been nothing but a load of calculated hooey designed to distract her from his real agenda.

"Well, over my dead body!" she muttered, flinging aside the icepack.

The door swung open and rubber-soled shoes whispered across the floor. "Stubborn, aren't you?" the nurse remarked, sizing up the situation. "What's it going to take to convince you I know best—another crack on the head?"

"I'm in a hurry."

The nurse pursed her lips and shrugged. "Okay. Feel free to get up and leave."

"Finally!" Heaving a sigh of relief, Camille sat up and swung her legs over the side of the gurney.

Big mistake! The walls tilted, the overhead light swung crazily, and what her stomach was doing didn't bear thinking about. Defeated, she fell back against the pillow.

"Ex…actly!" Cordless telephone flat on her hand, the nurse stood sentinel, a ruthless prison guard disguised as a ministering angel. "Ready to make that call now?"

Refusing to give in to the tears of panic stretching her control to the limit because she knew, once she started crying, she'd never stop, Camille considered the only two options open. She could call her parents, confident that regardless of the harsh words she'd flung at them, they'd rush to her aid, or she could call Fran.

The nurse tapped her foot impatiently. "Well, sweetie, what's it going to be?"

She had a blinding headache, her stomach was queasy, and her life was a mess, all of which, Camille decided, left her with only one real option. Meekly, she took the phone and dialed Fran's number. At least *she* wouldn't say "I told you so."

Nor did she waste time asking questions. Like the good friend she was, she listened to Camille's brief explanation and said only, "Sit tight. I'll be there in half an hour."

"You'll be feeling more like yourself by then," the nurse said, when Camille relayed the message. "Keep the icepack in place, and I'll bring you some hot tea."

In fact, it was nearly an hour before Fran showed up. "The parking's the pits at this hour," she explained. "Then I had trouble finding this room. Sorry, Camille. I know you must be itching to get out of here, but don't worry about Jeremy. I phoned Nori and told her to bring him over to our place for dinner. I didn't think you'd feel up to cooking, so Adam's making barbecued ribs for all of us."

Light-headed again, but from relief this time, Camille eased her feet into her shoes and collected her handbag and jacket from the counter. Apart from being a bit weak at the knees, she felt almost normal again.

"Keep an eye on her," the nurse advised Fran, ushering

them out of the supply room. "She's been checked over by one of our staff doctors and doesn't seem to have suffered any serious concussion, but she did take quite a fall and shouldn't be left alone tonight. Here's a list of things to watch for. If you have any concerns, call her family doctor."

"Will do." Fran tucked the sheet of paper into her purse and turned to Camille. "Ready to go?"

She'd been ready for well over an hour, the need to see her son growing more urgent with each passing second. Not until she could hold his warm, solid little body in her arms and see for herself that he was safe, would she be able to relax. Without waiting for Fran, she started down the corridor, certain there was nothing in the world that could stop her headlong rush to freedom.

Nothing, that was, except finding herself in the middle of another nightmare. As she drew level with Rita Osborne's room, the door opened and Michael came out looking absolutely shattered.

There was no avoiding him, and no pretending he hadn't seen her, so she stood her ground and drew on the last reserves of her pride to get her past this final hurdle. "Hello, Michael," she said.

He stared at her as if he'd seen a ghost, then made a visible effort to pull himself together. "What the devil are you doing here, Camille?"

"I came to see Rita," she said. "Your wife, remember?"

Leaning against the wall, he dragged a weary hand over his face and try though she might to harden her heart, Camille couldn't help feeling sorry for him. He stared at his feet a moment, then lifted his gaze to her face. His blue eyes were bruised dark blue-black with pain and grief. "I can't deal with you right now," he said bleakly. "It'll have to wait."

Her pity evaporated in less time than it took to blink. *He* was giving *her* the brush-off, after all his duplicity? "I can't deal with you at all," she replied, the words chipping out of her mouth as hard as granite. "Not now, not ever."

Fran caught up to her just in time to hear her remark, took one look at her face, another at Michael's, and said, "I don't pretend to understand what's going down between the two of you, but I do suggest that this is not the place to sort it out. Michael, you look very upset. If you need someone to talk to, you know where to reach us. Camille, we're leaving. Now."

And with that she strong-armed Camille the rest of the way down the hall and around the corner to the elevators.

Whenever Camille had needed her, Fran had always been there, loyal and steadfast to the end, but patience wasn't her strongest suit. All the way down to the main floor and out to where she'd left the car, she kept her peace, but her curiosity was nearing boiling point. Camille knew it but she couldn't bring herself to confide in her friend. She huddled in the passenger seat, still too dazed with shock to put her thoughts into any sort of order, let alone share them, even with someone as sympathetic as she knew Fran would be.

They were approaching the Bay Bridge when Fran finally broke the silence. "Okay, Camille, if you're not going to volunteer, I'm going to pry. I didn't raise a peep when you phoned to say you were at St. Mary's and needed a ride home. I simply jumped in my car and came racing to your rescue. The least you can do is explain why. We can skip over the fact that you fainted for no apparent reason and now have a lump on your forehead that leaves you looking a bit like a unicorn, and go straight to the reason you were ready to rip Michael's throat out in full view of hospital staff. What the hell's got you in such a state?"

Camille sifted through all the possible answers: he's married; he's a liar; he's an adulterer. But in the end, only one really mattered. "He's Jeremy's father."

Fran swerved and narrowly missed sideswiping a car in the next lane. "That's insane!"

"But true, nevertheless. He's married to Rita Osborne. He's the abusive husband who abandoned her when she was pregnant."

"Did *he* tell you that?"

"He didn't have to. I caught him red-handed playing the devoted husband to his dying wife." She stared out of the window, the wheels of her mind spinning frantically. "Fran, I need to ask another favor."

"Well, sure." She sounded as if she'd been poleaxed. "Ask away."

"Will you please let Nori and Jeremy stay at your cottage in Bodega Bay for a few days?"

"Camille, all three of you can stay there for as long as you like, you know that."

"I have to stay at home. That's where he'll come looking."

"He? You mean, Michael?"

"Who else? The only reason he came here to begin with was to find his son. Now that he has, it's pretty obvious what his next move will be."

"He doesn't have a snowball's hope in hell of ever getting his hands on Jeremy, if that's what's worrying you."

"Don't be so sure," she said, recalling how persistently he'd quizzed her on the details leading up to Jeremy's adoption, and how artlessly she'd given him the ammunition he'd so obviously been seeking.

There might be, he'd said, that night by the river when she'd told him there was no way Rita Osborne's delinquent husband could ever take Jeremy away from her. *Given the fact that your husband opted out of the responsibilities he deliberately undertook, a court might look very favorably on a natural father's claim to his blood child.*

"You've got every reason to be furious with him, Camille, I grant you that," Fran said, "but don't let your imagination run wild. He might have a lot to answer for, but he doesn't strike me as a kidnapper."

Never trust a stranger, Camille. You're asking for trouble if you do....

"He wants Jeremy, Fran. I know that for a fact."

Fran flung her a startled look. "You mean he actually came out and admitted as much?"

"Yes. I just didn't realize it until now. But everything he's said and done since he first came to town points to that. The evidence was there all the time, if only I'd known what to look for. Instead, I let myself be taken in by his smile and his kisses. I even...."

Despair at how easily she'd fallen into the trap he'd laid dammed the words in her throat and she couldn't finish. Couldn't bring herself to admit what an utter fool she'd been. But she'd said enough to lead Fran to all the right conclusions.

"Are you telling me the two of you made love, Camille?"

"Not quite." She bit her lip and cursed the tears stinging her eyes. "According to him, all we did was have sex. Unfortunately, I chose to read more into it than that. Silly me, huh?"

"Don't be so hard on yourself. I've seen the way he looks at you and I'd bet money that he's not exactly...let's see, how do I put this delicately? He's not exactly *unmoved* by your charms. That ought to bring you some comfort."

"I don't see how."

"Well, add it up for yourself, dearie! You're the adoptive

mother of his son, he wants to play an active role in his son's life, and the pair of you are halfway in love with each other. If that doesn't balance out to the ideal equation for a marriage of convenience, I don't know what does!''

''You seem to forget that one part of the equation is already married to someone else.''

Fran blew out a frustrated breath. ''It's not that I've forgotten so much as I'm having a hard time believing it. Are you sure you didn't misunderstand?''

''I know what I heard, and I know what I saw. He's married, and he loves his wife.''

''You're certain of that?''

Caught in the vicious treadmill of memory, the words she'd overheard echoed relentlessly inside her head.

I'll sit with your wife…

I love you, Mike…

I love you, too, honey….

''Absolutely,'' she said.

Three hours before, the sun had rung down the curtain for Kay in a great orange ball of splendor. Now, nothing but a carpet of more stars than he could count in a lifetime filled the sky. No mist crept up from the ocean to shroud him in privacy as he stared emptily out at the view; no sympathetic cloud shadowed the bright moon.

Not that he gave a damn who saw him or what they might think of a man slumped on a park bench, with only a plastic bag containing a dead woman's personal effects for company. He was past caring about anything at all except the wicked waste of a life burnt out long before its time.

It was all very fine for the priest who'd administered the last rites to tell him that she'd found peace at last. *He* hadn't been the one who'd stood by helpless to erase the fear in her eyes before she sank into final unconsciousness. Nor had he been the one she'd turned to at the last and begged, "Take care of my baby, Michael...promise me you will."

He would, of course. But he didn't fool himself that it was going to be easy. No one had been able to tell him how Camille had found her way into Kay's room. Nor did it much matter beside the far greater issue of her having discovered the truth from someone other than himself.

Superimposed over his grief for Kay, the memory of Camille's pained shock when she'd come face-to-face with him in the hospital corridor bedeviled him. What he wouldn't have given for the right to take her in his arms and just hold her without any need for words.

Tomorrow, there were arrangements to be made—the tying off of all the loose ends still connecting Kay to a world where she no longer belonged. He'd take care of them first because there was no one else to do the job. Then, in a few days, when he had himself under better control, he'd go to Camille and find a way to atone for the hurt he'd dealt her, and at the same time try to honor his last promise to Kay.

It was the least he could do. Even though she'd died without his ever discovering why she'd cast him in the role of villainous husband, his anger had long since been swallowed up by pity. Her wrongdoing had caught up with her in the end and exacted a terrible price.

Once Jeremy and Nori were safely stashed in the Knowltons' cottage up the coast, Camille waited, knowing it was a matter of time only before Michael showed up. She kept the gates closed, the security system armed, and for three days paced the house, steeling herself for the showdown. Rehearsing what she'd say. Promising herself she wouldn't be swayed by anything he might throw at her: not by outrage or misery, and most of all not by sweet talk.

Then, just after ten on the morning of the fourth day, the intercom buzzed and her heart rate went into overdrive. But the closed-circuit television screen showed only the maintenance crew come to clean the pool. As soon as they left, she activated the remote lock to secure the gates again.

If there was to be a final confrontation, she intended to take charge of it from the outset and be ready for him. He'd caught her off guard for the last time. Or so she thought.

But he tricked her again, appearing so silently from the shrubbery surrounding the pool deck that she wasn't even aware of his presence until his shadow fell across the open book in her lap.

"Before you raise the alarm, I come in peace," he said, dropping into the chaise next to hers. "And if you're wondering how I got past all that fancy electronic equipment undetected, I parked down the road and slipped through the gates on foot when that van left. I knew you wouldn't let me in otherwise."

He wore black denim jeans and a short-sleeved white shirt unbuttoned at the neck. His face looked thinner, giving cleaner emphasis to the hard line of his jaw. Furrows of fatigue radiated from the corners of his eyes. His mouth was curved with sorrow, and the sun glinted off a few threads of silver in the hair at his temples.

He looked so wretched, so utterly defeated, that she was reminded of a beautiful wounded angel condemned to a hell she couldn't begin to imagine, and it was all she could do to remain impervious to his pain.

"Why wouldn't I let you in?" she said, finding some solace in the fact that she didn't sound a fraction as disconcerted as she felt. "I'm not afraid of you. If anything I pity you. Even a man of your shabby morals deserves a hearing, guilty though you are of the most contemptible deceit."

"I doubt anything I have to say is going to cut much ice with you at this stage, Camille."

"I doubt it, too. But you are the man who once told me confession is good for the soul, are you not?"

He sighed and looked around, his expression so wretched that despite everything he'd done, a twinge of pity stirred the cold ashes of the passion he'd once aroused in her. Before it took too firm a hold, she reminded herself that the hell he was in was of his own making and if she let him draw her into it, too, she deserved all the misery she'd undoubtedly reap.

Affecting an indifference she was far from feeling, she said, "Well? Is there *anything* you have to say, or shall I call the police and have you arrested for trespassing?"

If he'd come back with an apology, or cut to the chase and simply told her the truth, no matter how ugly it might be, she might have been able to hang on to her dignity.

But he did neither. Instead, he cast a searching glance over the garden and said, "Is Jeremy here?"

CHAPTER NINE

HE WASN'T off to the best start.

"No, Jeremy is not here!" she fairly shrieked, bolting out of the chair and flying at him.

Before she could rake her fingernails down his face, he fended her off with one hand and said, "Calm down, for Pete's sake! The only reason I asked was I didn't want to chance him overhearing us again."

"So you say!" she spat. "But we both know that's just a smokescreen to get you what you're really after."

She was petrified, he realized. Her eyes were huge as saucers, their pupils dilated with fear. "Honey, I don't know why you think I'm here—"

"Don't you 'honey' me!" she said, aiming a kick at his shins which he avoided by calling on soccer skills he hadn't used in a long time. "I'm not your 'honey' and I never was. Save it for your wife Rita, though if she's as easily taken in by your endearments as I was, I feel sorry for her."

"In fact she was my ex-wife, but it's a moot point now. She died on Sunday afternoon, moments before I ran into you outside her room."

He conveyed the news less to arouse sympathy than to deflate her anger because, as things now stood, trying to engage in a reasonable conversation was a lost cause.

The ploy worked. The fight went out of her and her voice was hushed when she said, "I'm sorry. I could see how ill she was, poor thing. I'm sure you must be very grieved."

"I am," he admitted. "A lot more than I expected, given

that we've been divorced nearly five years and hadn't been in touch once in all that time until very recently.''

"Oh, please!" The fire in her eyes erupted again as quickly as it had died down. "If the only reason you're here is to add another lie to the pile you've already told, I don't want to hear it."

He frowned, puzzled. "What lie? You've known from the beginning that I'd been married, Camille. Why are you making such an issue of it now?"

"Maybe because I heard you tell her you love her. *And* I heard the nurse refer to her as your wife. In my book, neither adds up to your being divorced."

"At the stage she was at, I'd have told her whatever I thought she wanted to hear because, by then, it was *all* I could do for her," he said. "Sure she'd made some mistakes and done some terrible things, but she was already paying for them big time and I didn't see it as my job to add to her load. There comes a time when a guy has to move past all the anger and resentment that's been eating him alive. For me, that time came on Sunday.

"As for the nurse calling her my wife...." He shrugged. "It was a harmless mistake on her part and I'm sorry if it bothered you, but frankly I had bigger things on my mind right then than setting a comparative stranger straight on my marital status. I'd have thought, considering what you'd just learned, that you would have had, too."

"Adultery isn't something I can just brush aside as being of no consequence."

She was sticking to her position of woman wronged, but it was costing her. He could tell by the way her tone lost some of its starch, plus the fact that she couldn't quite meet his gaze.

"We didn't commit adultery, Camille," he said, lessening his hold on her wrist and snagging her fingers in his.

"I know I've kept things from you, but I'm being completely up-front with you on this."

He'd have done better to keep his distance. She snatched her hand away as if he'd stubbed out a burning cigarette on it. "I can't imagine why you think I'd believe anything coming out of your mouth!"

He raised both arms in surrender and backed off a couple of yards. "All right, let me put it to you like this—if a stranger tells you what an adorable kid Jeremy is, do you feel obligated to point out that he's adopted?"

"Don't be ridiculous! Of course I don't."

"You confide it only to people who matter?"

She flushed. "Oh, all right, you've made your point! So you weren't lying about being divorced. Congratulations, I'm sure! But that hardly mitigates your other deceptions."

"I'm aware of that," he said. "And if you think they haven't weighed heavily on my conscience for quite some time now, you don't know me as well as you think you do."

"I don't know you at all!" she said scornfully. "You never intended that I should, or you'd have been open with me from the start."

"How so? By marching up to you the day we met and saying, 'Hi, that's my son you're parking on the merry-go-round, and if it's all the same to you I'd like to get to know him, so how about I come to your house tomorrow and we'll work out a visitation schedule?'"

"At least I'd have known where I stood. We might have been able to arrive at some sort of agreement."

"Come off it, Camille! I'm supposed to be the liar here, not you. You'd have tried to have me thrown in jail, and we both know it. And I can't say I'd have blamed you, given the story Kay had fed you."

She eyed him suspiciously. "Who's Kay?"

"My ex. Until she married me and took my name, she was Rita Kay Osborne, but everyone called her Kay. She didn't start using the name Rita until after the divorce."

"Probably because she wanted to disassociate herself from you as thoroughly as possible. You were a rotten husband."

"I'm sure I made my share of mistakes but contrary to what she might have led you to believe, walking away from my son isn't one of them. If I'd known she was pregnant, I'd have provided for her and the baby."

"And?"

It was pretty clear what else she was asking, and he wasn't about to compromise his integrity any more than he already had, even if this was the one time she'd have preferred him to lie. "And he'd never have been put up for adoption on the black market."

"I *knew* it!" Her voice trembled pitifully and it was all he could do not to haul her close and kiss her fears into oblivion. "This is where you've been headed all along, isn't it? It's why you seduced me—because you thought, if you softened me up, I'd let you…trample roughshod over my entire world."

"That isn't why, Camille," he said. "If you believe nothing else, know that the one thing I've most wanted to avoid is hurting you."

"Well, you didn't succeed!" she cried, her eyes streaming. "You've taken my life and chopped it up into little pieces. And you're not done yet, are you?"

Dealing effectively with a woman's tears was something he'd never mastered. Despite her Irish ancestry, his mother's equable temperament had seldom crumbled in the face of adversity, and Kay's way of retaliation when things hadn't gone her way had been the silent treatment. At his wit's end, he said, "Now what sin have I committed? For

Pete's sake, Camille, it seems I can't do anything right with you, no matter how hard I try.''

''Oh, stop it! *Stop it!* I know why you're here, and it's got nothing to do with trying to make things right. You've come to take my son away from me.''

''Huh?''

He must have looked as stunned as he felt, because she came at him again, all spitting fury. ''What's the matter, Michael? Do words escape you for once? My goodness, when someone beats you to the punch, you're not quite as nimble with the glib replies, are you?''

Unless he found a way to calm her down, she was going to tip over the edge into full-blown hysteria, something he *knew* he'd never handle. ''Sweetheart,'' he said, trying once again to take her in his arms and placate her, ''you've got it all wrong.''

She slapped him away. ''Save it, Michael. You're going to have to come up with something a lot more original than a repeat performance of the same old smooth moves if you seriously expect me to hand my child over to you. I'll see you in hell first!''

''I have no intention of trying to take Jeremy away from you.''

''Then why are you here?''

''Because I hoped we could behave like the two mature adults we're supposed to be. I hoped that, instead of leaping to irrational conclusions, you'd at least listen while I offered the explanations I know are long overdue. But given your present frame of mind, it doesn't look as if that's going to happen.''

''No, it isn't,'' she said. ''I'm not feeling very rational right now. I'm feeling distinctly threatened because I've come to realize that, with you, there's always a hidden agenda.''

"Not anymore, Camille," he said, his patience at an end. The last few days had been rough; the nights even rougher. Answers he'd hoped to find, Kay had taken to the grave, and the ensuing frustration was wearing him down. "The gloves are off. You're looking at a man who promised a dying woman that he'd take care of her son, and I'm telling you up-front that it's a promise I intend to keep."

"He's not her son!" she cried, her face contorting in pain. "He's mine. And I can look after him without any help from you, so take your promises and choke on them!"

He could have tried persuasion. He could have soothed her ruffled feathers by spelling out his intentions and thus proving that he had nothing diabolical up his sleeve. But when a woman had made up her mind not to listen, no matter how reasonable the idea being presented, a man's best recourse was to keep his answer short and succinct. So he planted his feet apart, folded his arms, and drowned her out with a resounding, "No!"

Her mouth fell open in pure shock, leaving him to suspect that not many people had dared say "no" to her in the past. That she managed to look adorable, whether she was sobbing, raging or gaping, hadn't escaped his notice either, but it was fast losing its charm. He was tired of being manipulated by the women in his life. It had been too late to do much about it by the time he learned what Kay had been up to behind his back, but he was damned if he was going to let Camille lead him around by the nose.

"You don't have any choice," she told him, recovering quickly. "You don't have the right to come charging into his life and taking over. I'm his legal parent, not you. I've got the papers to prove it."

"Don't make me play hardball, Camille," he said softly. "We both know I've got a strong case, should I choose to pursue the matter through the courts. As for your having papers!'' He let out a snort of disgust. ''Hell, we're talking about a child here, not a pedigreed pooch, though I suppose, given that you cut your teeth on the theory that money can buy just about anything you set your heart on, it shouldn't surprise me that you see my son as just another commodity.''

At that, the little witch stepped close and poked him hard in the chest with her finger. Twice. Cripes! ''Well, it certainly didn't take long for you to show your true colors, did it, you great overgrown bully?'' she seethed. ''I can't believe I ever bought your Mr. Nice Guy act.''

''I'm exactly the same person I've always been, Camille. A man cheated out of knowing his own son by my desperate former wife and your sleazy excuse of a husband.''

''*Ex*-husband!''

''Now, perhaps,'' he amended, pretty steamed himself by then. ''But he wasn't when he drew up that shady adoption agreement, was he? He was married to you, and you both stood to gain by the arrangement he made. Trouble was, he couldn't live with what he'd done and took refuge in the bottle. But you never had a problem, did you? Even though, by your own admission, you thought the whole deal smelled to high heaven, you just held your nose and kept right on playing the perfect mother and poor, long-suffering wife.''

He was out of line and he knew it. From the way she stiffened in outrage, she knew it, too, and probably would have decked him if the ding-dong tone of the security alarm hadn't warned her that someone had entered the house through one of the perimeter doors.

Flinging him a last poisonous glare, she crossed the pool deck and started up the steps leading to the house. By the time she reached the top with him close behind, the Japanese nanny and Jeremy had appeared on the terrace.

He looked flushed and miserable, and the nanny looked worried.

"So sorry not to wait for your call before we came back," she said, giving a little bow, "but Jeremy's cold grew much worse overnight and this morning he complained of an earache, so I thought it best to bring him home."

Stooping, Camille held out her arms. The little guy stumbled to her and buried his face against her skirt. She brushed a soothing hand down the side of his cheek and under his jaw. "You did the right thing, Nori," she said, nodding reassuringly at the nanny. "He's burning up with fever. Run a cool bath so we can sponge him down, will you, while I place a call to Doctor Hythe?"

The nanny scuttled away.

"Probably an ear infection," Michael said, trying to be helpful.

Camille looked at him as if he were something that had crawled out of the woodwork. "And how would you know?"

"I might not know much about being a father, but I'm a pretty experienced uncle and I've seen this happen before when a kid his age gets a cold that starts acting up. If I'm right, the sooner he's on antibiotics, the sooner he'll start to feel better."

"You think I don't already know that?"

"I'm beginning to wonder. Why else would you be wasting time arguing the point? Here, let me take him while you make that phone call."

"Absolutely not!" Small, perfect breasts heaving, she pulled Jeremy into the shelter of her arm and held him glued to her side as if she feared he might physically tear the boy away from her. "Nori!" she cried, so much terror in her voice that Mike winced.

Cripes, what kind of ogre did she think he was?

The nanny reappeared on silent feet, a huge bath towel draped over one arm. Edging toward the door, Camille gave the child a gentle push. "Go with Nori, darling. Mommy'll be with you in a minute—as soon as she sees Mr. D'Alessandro off the premises."

"Forget it, Camille. I'm not going anywhere," Michael said, as the nanny trotted off with her charge.

"You're not getting your hands on my son, either," Camille informed him. "And just in case you're thinking of resorting to brute force, Nori holds a black belt in karate and don't think for a moment that she'll hesitate to use it if you try to interfere. You'll be flat on your back before you know what hit you."

It was the last and most ridiculous in a tired list of threats. "Will you for Pete's sake stop over-dramatizing and get your priorities straight!" he roared. "I've had it up to here with your nonsense, you hear? Like it or not, that's my boy we're talking about and I'm not about to be shoved aside like an old shoe when he obviously needs medical attention."

"I'm his mother—"

"And making a hopeless mess of the job right now, if you ask me!"

She drew herself up to her full five-feet-five or whatever, aristocratic nostrils flaring. "You really are an insulting boor, aren't you?"

"Honey, you have no idea the depths to which I can sink if I'm pushed far enough. But keep this up, and you'll find out soon enough."

Her gaze flickered, and she gnawed on her lip a moment. "Much though it galls me to admit it, you're right," she finally admitted. "Jeremy comes first. If you want to help, you can drive us to the clinic. We'll take my car. You'll

find the keys on a hook in the rear hall, next to the door
leading to the garage. I'll meet you at the front entrance in
ten minutes."

She didn't wait to hear his answer. She just left him to
find his way through the house to the area in question. She
might suffer all kinds of uncertainties in other areas of her
life, but put her in mother mode and she dished out orders
as if she owned the world.

They were headed home within the hour, complete with
prescribed medications for the ear infection he'd predicted,
and for all that she tried to hang on to her resentment,
Camille couldn't help being grateful that Michael was with
her. For so long, she'd had only herself to rely on in a
crisis. Having a man take charge, even of something as
simple as driving and parking the car so that she was free
to devote herself to Jeremy's needs, made such a difference
to the load she'd carried for the past three years.

Covertly, she glanced at him, searching for some physical likeness to Jeremy, but she could find nothing in the
stern profile of the man behind the wheel which in the least
resembled the sweet childish features of her son.

For that matter, there was nothing of the charming lover
she'd briefly known, either. A new and disconcerting side
of Michael had emerged, along with the truth of his identity. Underneath that sexy, easygoing exterior lurked the
toughness of a street fighter. It would not be wise to alien-
ate him, and wiser still not to let him see how afraid he
made her.

Wetting her lips nervously, she said, "Thank you for
caring enough to help us out when you already have so
much else on your mind."

"I thought I'd made it clear that nothing takes precedence over my son's well-being."

She almost cried out, *Don't you dare call him that!* But the shocking reality was, he and Jeremy were genetically linked and no amount of wishing it were otherwise was going to sever the connection. So rather than start another all-out war, she buried her objection in a cough and took a more diplomatic tack. "It might be best," she said, casting a cautious glance over her shoulder to make sure Jeremy couldn't overhear, "if you didn't say that in front of Jeremy."

"He's asleep," Michael informed her curtly. "Has been for the last ten minutes. He can't hear a thing."

"Still, if he should get any inkling of…who you are, it would confuse him terribly. He's already asked why he doesn't have a daddy."

"Well, now you can tell him that he does."

"No, Michael!" Dismayed, she clutched at his arm.

He shrugged her off as if she were as inconsequential as a gnat. "Then I will."

Terror rose up again, and try though she might, she couldn't contain it. "Please don't! He's too little to understand why."

"You mean to say you haven't taught him all about the birds and the bees yet?" A bitter smile touched his mouth. "Shame on you!"

"This isn't a joke."

The glance he flung at her was so weary and disillusioned, she could have wept. "Hell, Camille, right now I'll take my laughs any place I can find them."

"What I meant was, if you tell him you're his father, he'll want to know why you don't live with us. He's just a little boy, Michael. Don't expect him to believe you care about him unless you plan to be around to prove it."

He blinked and looked away. A sigh shook him. "I've

got to tell you, I don't know how I'm going to leave him, Camille. I wish there was a way—''

Had the seed Fran planted taken root without her knowing it, or was it the wretched misery which crossed Michael's face that made her blurt out rashly, ''Maybe there is. We could get married—purely for Jeremy's sake, of course. It might not be the ideal arrangement for you and me, but it's what's best for him that matters.''

The silence with which he greeted the suggestion was so lengthy and painful that she wished she could curl up into a ball and disappear. When she could bear the suspense of waiting for his reply not a second longer, she closed her eyes in an anguish of humiliation and mumbled, ''On second thought, it's a stupid idea. It would never work.''

Just as swiftly as her heart had sunk, it soared again when he said thoughtfully, ''Hold your horses. I haven't turned you down yet.''

She sucked in a breath, hardly daring to contemplate what it might mean if he were to say yes. Could they make a marriage work?

She could! She could do whatever it took to keep Jeremy with her and make him happy, including turning a blind eye to the fact that Michael probably wouldn't have looked at her twice if it weren't that she had something he desperately wanted.

So what if he wasn't in love with her? He was decent and kind and dependable. He didn't buckle in the face of adversity. He'd never put his own interests ahead of Jeremy's. And she'd lived with a weakling long enough to know that *they* were the qualities that really mattered, not how often he showered her with compliments or toasted her with champagne.

But to her disappointment, when he spoke again it had nothing to do with marriage or Jeremy. ''Strange,'' he said, slowing down to make the turn into her driveway. "I could have sworn I closed the gates when we left."

"You did," she said. "I distinctly remember it."

"But they're open now. Guess you must have company."

He was right. As they rounded the last curve in the drive, a gray Mercedes-Benz, one she recognized with sinking dismay, loomed into view at the far end of the guest parking area next to the house.

The minute Michael brought the car to a stop, she leapt out and without waiting for him to lift Jeremy from the back seat, raced up the steps to the front door just as Nori, who must have heard their arrival, pulled it open. "They phoned," she said, anticipating the question before Camille could ask, "and although I tried to put them off, when they heard you'd taken Jeremy to the doctor, they insisted on coming over."

They would! Taking orders from a nanny, even one as impeccably polite and respectful as Nori, wasn't in their nature.

"It can't be helped. As long as they don't know Michael was with me—"

Nori looked distressed. "They already do. They saw his car on the side of the road and recognized it."

So the troops were in place, waiting to mount another offensive. And Michael, with a sleepy Jeremy in his arms, was climbing the steps and about to walk into the line of fire.

"Where are they now?"

"Having coffee on the terrace."

Desperate to avoid what would undoubtedly be a disastrous confrontation, Camille said, "Okay, here's what we'll do. You get Michael to take Jeremy upstairs to bed and ask him to stay with him until I come up, and I'll get rid of my parents.''

It wasn't an ideal solution, but it was the best she could come up with at such short notice because she knew without bothering to ask that Michael wouldn't just deposit Jeremy on the doorstep, then leave. Nor did she want him to, not with the question of marriage still hanging in the balance.

"We heard," her mother started in, the second Camille stepped out to the terrace. "And it goes without saying that we are horrified."

"Don't be," Camille said, deliberately misunderstanding. "It's just a mild ear infection—nothing serious. He'll be back to his usual self in no time at all."

"We aren't talking about Jeremy," her father said. "Camille, we hoped that when you discovered the extent of that man's mischief, you'd have the good sense to send him packing."

"*That man* happens to be Jeremy's father, Dad. Even if I wanted to, I doubt I could keep him away from his son."

From the thunderstruck expressions on both their faces, it was obvious that their private investigator hadn't done quite as thorough a job as her parents thought.

"That's preposterous!" her father exclaimed.

"Nevertheless, it's the truth."

"He's no such thing and if he told you he is, it's just to cover up the fact that he's had another woman on the side all the time he's been inveigling himself into your life. The man is an outright liar."

"And a money-grubbing opportunist," her mother put in.

Her father waved that observation aside as if it went without saying that *of course* money was at the root of the whole problem. "What I don't understand, Camille, is why a woman of your intelligence would swallow such an implausible story.''

"Because I found irrefutable proof that it's true, that's why. The woman he was visiting in St. Mary's was Rita Osborne and if the name doesn't ring a bell, it should. She was Jeremy's birth mother.''

"So? What's that got to do with anything?''

"Michael was her ex-husband.''

Her father turned faintly purple and swung his head like a wild animal sniffing out a hidden enemy. "Are you telling us he's the lout who left her on the street with nothing but the clothes on her back?''

"No, because that never happened. It was just one of many in Rita's web of lies. I'm telling you he was denied the knowledge that he'd fathered Jeremy and only recently discovered the truth. Unless we can come to some sort of amicable agreement, I'm terrified he'll try to have Jeremy's adoption rendered invalid.'' She paused to let that information sink in before delivering what she knew they'd find the most shocking news of all. "Which is why I've asked him to marry me. I can think of no other way to protect my son from an ugly and damaging custody battle.''

"Dear heaven!'' her mother squeaked, falling into the nearest chair. "Camille, you've lost your mind. You need professional help!''

"Because I'm prepared to do whatever it takes to prevent my son's life from being turned upside down? I don't think so, Mother.''

"Have you no understanding of the ramifications involved if you go ahead with this harebrained scheme?'' her father bellowed. "At present, Michael D'Alessandro owns nothing but a two-bit construction operation somewhere in Canada. But throw in your lot with him, and *your* assets become *his* assets. He marries you, he takes you away from us—to a foreign country where the law will favor him. And once he's established parental rights to Jeremy, he can divorce you and *you*'ll be the one left with nothing worth having.''

''Not necessarily. We could draw up a prenuptial agreement.'' She flung out her hands. ''It's not ideal, I agree, but it's something I can live with, and it's a lot better than spending the rest of my life looking over my shoulder and afraid to let Jeremy out of my sight.''

''So he gets a rich wife, and a son he doesn't deserve—''

''And I get peace of mind. You can't put a price tag·on that, Dad.''

''You'll be selling yourself into bondage,'' her mother said, ''and I think you'll find that to be quite a hefty price tag in the long run.''

''I'm prepared to make whatever sacrifice is necessary to keep my son, including selling my soul to the devil if I have to.''

''You don't have to go to that extreme,'' her father insisted. ''I'll hire the best lawyers in the city to make sure you don't lose him. And if that vagabond tries to take my grandson out of the state, I'll have him arrested for kidnapping and thrown in jail.''

''Your father's right, Camille,'' her mother said. ''Forget this crazy idea. Michael D'Alessandro will never make you happy.'' She shuddered fastidiously. ''He's too commonplace. Too…earthy.''

''Better listen to Mommy, Camille,'' Michael said from the doorway behind her. ''I'm all of that and more. It'd be a real step down for a princess like you to wind up married to a peasant like me. You'd be sacrificing everything your little heart's been trained to hold dear.''

CHAPTER TEN

THE fact that he'd snuck up on them unobserved did nothing to increase his stock with Glenda Younge. Lurching out of her chair as if she'd found a viper in her drawers, she squawked, "And how long have you been listening in?"

"Long enough," he said, dismissing her and addressing his next remark to Camille. "Not that I'd dream of deflecting you from more important issues, but just in case you're interested, Jeremy's medication is taking effect already. His temperature's down and he's fallen asleep again."

She had the grace to look somewhat sheepish. "Of course I'm interested. Thank you for keeping an eye on him for me."

"You left him alone with Jeremy?" the dragon lady cried. "My heavens, Camille, you've just finished telling us you're afraid the man might kidnap the child! What were you thinking?"

"I never said that, Mother. What I said was—"

"That you're prepared to do whatever it takes to protect your place in his life, including marrying me if you have to." Mike grimaced. "I'm overwhelmed! The lengths to which you'll go and the sacrifices you're prepared to make, all in the name of maternal dedication, are admirable, Camille."

"Well, there's no use pretending it would be a love match, is there?" she said, turning pink. "We've both been down that road before and ended precisely nowhere, so we might as well call a spade a spade and admit it would be purely a marriage of convenience."

155

"You're missing the point, my dear. In common with every other contract, a marriage of convenience requires one essential component to make it work. How many divorces is it going to take, Camille, before you figure out that trust between the parties involved is the glue that holds a partnership together?"

"If I didn't trust you, do you really think I'd have suggested we share responsibility for Jeremy?"

"Sure I do. Your history speaks for itself. You used Todd to get Jeremy and now you're willing to use me to keep him. And just in case there's a loophole you've overlooked, you'll get me to sign a prenup agreement to protect all your other interests. Talk about covering your ass!"

"Look here, Mr. D'Alessandro," the father cut in. "It's unfortunate that you overheard things not intended for your ears, but you do yourself no favors by browbeating my daughter, particularly not since she is disposed to be generous in allowing you some access to her son."

"*My* son, Mr. Younge."

"You gave him up."

"I did no such thing, nor am I about to now."

"Be reasonable, man! Whether or not you knowingly rescinded your parental rights is immaterial after all this time. You don't have a prayer of getting the adoption order overturned."

"I'm not sure he knows what 'rescind' means," the mother whispered ostentatiously.

"I know what it means," Mike informed her. "Now let me ask you a question. Do you know what I mean when I tell you I'm tired of having to listen to you quacking on about something which is none of your bloody business?"

She looked so scandalized, anyone would have thought he'd just ripped open a raincoat and exposed himself.

"Camille is our daughter," she gasped, fanning herself with her outsize purse. "That makes her our business."

"She's a grown woman, even if she doesn't always act like one. She's got a mind of her own and it's about time you let her use it."

"She's too distraught to think straight, and it's all your fault. I knew you were trouble the minute I laid eyes on you, insinuating yourself into our lives and pretending you were someone of consequence when the truth is, you barely have two cents to rub together."

"Be quiet, Mother," Camille said, with a lot more command than he'd expected. "Michael's right. This is none of your business."

Her father jumped in again then, with another two bits worth of unasked-for advice. "Perhaps not, but you'd do well to look at the product before you rush to put money down on your purchase. You heard the way he spoke to your mother just now, and you've seen for yourself how he managed to bamboozle you with his lies. You'd still be believing every word he says if we hadn't opened your eyes to the truth. Well, a leopard doesn't change his spots, Camille. If you don't think he'll subject you to the same verbal abuse he flung at your mother, or continue to prevaricate whenever it suits his purpose, then you deserve all the trouble you'll be buying."

"Better listen to the old man," Mike advised her mockingly. "He's so sure he knows better than anyone else about everything from soup to nuts that if creating the world had been left to him, he'd probably have had it finished in half the time it took God to do the job."

"I certainly know all about men like you," her father snapped. "Ill-bred, uneducated, posing as an entrepreneur when all you're really looking for is a free ride to easy street."

"I don't know where you got your information—"

"I had you investigated."

"Then you didn't get your money's worth. I'm not interested in getting into a spitting match with you, but if the man you hired had done his job properly, you'd know that I'm a university honors graduate with a degree in structural engineering, and my entrepreneurial skills have just landed me a contract worth a cool six point five million dollars— not enough to match the Younge fortune, perhaps, but more than enough to buy the help I need to reclaim my son."

That knocked some of the wind out of the old man's sails. He hemmed and hawed, adjusted the knot in his tie, and exchanged a glance with his wife whose mental calculator was practically clicking aloud. "They're accomplishments worthy of note, certainly—assuming, of course, that you're speaking the truth for once."

"You can verify it easily enough with a phone call to the University of British Columbia. As for my being ill-bred, my father might have been a working man and my mother a housewife, but I can promise you that if you'd ever been invited into their home, as I was invited into this one today, you'd have been treated with the utmost courtesy and respect—not because you've got money coming out of your keister and think that makes you better than everyone else, but because that's the way they always treated guests. Not that I expect you to appreciate such a foreign concept."

"There's no need to be sarcastic, young man. If we've misjudged you, we're sorry. It's possible you're more deserving than we originally thought."

His tone suggested it was probable pigs would fly before he'd make such a gross error in judgment, and swallowing cyanide a hell of a lot more palatable than having to admit he might be wrong.

If he hadn't been so ticked off, Mike might have laughed at the man's discomfiture. "Let's not go overboard with the compliments," he said. "We both know you think I'm pond scum."

"At last we agree on something. Sadly, the conferring of a university degree does not, of itself, endow a man with breeding."

"Well, heaven forbid I should prove you wrong yet again, so here's one more thing for you to chew on. I'm also a bulldog when it comes to protecting what's mine."

"That sounds like a threat, Mr. D'Alessandro."

"Read it any way you like, but know this—from where I stand, leaving my boy to fall under your kind of influence and doing nothing to counteract it, marks me as a negligent father, and that's not a label I care to have hanging around my neck."

"What are you saying, Michael?" Camille asked, her voice brimming with alarm.

He daren't look at her because he knew if he did, he'd cave in. She reminded him of a lovely, fragile butterfly batting its wings frantically against the net closing over it. His every instinct was to rescue her, to spare her injury, to let her fly free without let or hindrance. But doing that would mean more than breaking his promise to Kay; it would mean corrupting the principles which formed the lodestar of his existence. And if he did that, he'd never be able to live with himself.

"Your parents don't want me breathing the same rarified air as you, Camille. And I don't think you've got the moral fiber to go against their wishes. So I'm turning down your proposal. You might be desperate but I'm not, and I sure don't need the in-laws from hell playing vigilante on your behalf. If I ever marry again, it'll be to a woman able to stand on her own two feet and who sees me as something other than a monster who has to be appeased at any price.''

He was at the front door before she caught up with him. ''I've never thought of you that way,'' she cried, hanging on to his arm. ''Please don't punish me for my parents' mistakes.''

''I might be a trusting schmuck who got taken to the cleaners once, but it isn't going to happen a second time. You're cut from the same cloth they are, Camille, and you want to know what clinched it for me? That you were a party to a private investigation all the time you were kissing up to me.''

''I wasn't a party to it,'' she whispered hollowly. ''Not until the end, and only then because my curiosity got the better of me. When I went to the hospital, all I had to go on was a floor and room number, nothing else. I had no idea I'd find Rita, or that she was your ex-wife. I'd never have made the connection if it hadn't been for the photos of Jeremy.''

He wiped his hand down his face, all the weeks of subterfuge combined with the misery of the last week leaving him suddenly weary. ''You know what, it really doesn't matter anymore. The cat's out of the bag and nothing you or your parents can do is going to stuff it back in again. I have a son and there's no way I'm letting you or anyone else cut me out of his life. I've already missed too much of it.''

''So you're going to tear him away from everything dear and familiar, just to satisfy your need for revenge? My goodness, whatever happened to sweet reason and rational discussion, Michael?''

''It went the way of trust.''

She shifted from one foot to the other and made a concerted effort to hang on to her control, but she was close to breaking point and he knew he had to get away. He could be as merciless as the next guy when it came to fighting for what he believed in and defending his rights, but driving Camille over the edge—hell, that was more than he could handle.

"You'll be hearing from me," he said, yanking the door open, "but if, before then, you need to get in touch, I'm staying at the Portland. I expect to be kept informed of Jeremy's progress. If he gets worse, let me know immediately."

He made his tone intentionally brusque and it seemed to do the trick. She wrestled her emotions into line and glared at him from eyes brilliant with unshed tears. "You're certainly showing your true colors now, aren't you? Whatever happened to that nice man who—"

"Haven't you heard, Camille? Nice guys finish last. And I don't like losing so from now on, you'll be playing by my rules."

"And exactly what will that involve?"

"I'll call later on tonight and let you know. I'll tell you this much, though. Do yourself a favor and get rid of your folks before then because I've had about as much of their interference as I can stomach. This is between you and me, and if you persist in involving them, I can promise you you aren't going to be happy with the outcome."

He phoned at half past eight and foregoing any social discourse, leapt straight to the point. "I assume you're alone?"

Not a trace of warmth or humanity colored his words. This was the voice of a man well used to emerging the winner in the dog-eat-dog world of business.

"I'm alone," she said, grateful that he couldn't see the pain she knew was written all over her face.

She wanted the other Michael back; the one she'd known before. Why couldn't they have fallen in love at first sight and eloped to the Dominican Republic before her parents' well-meant interference threw everything out of kilter? His being Jeremy's father wouldn't have mattered then. The three of them would've been one big happy family regardless.

"How is Jeremy?"

"Much better. Asleep."

"Good. I'll be flying home tomorrow, but I'll leave a number where I can be reached any time, night or day. Keep me posted. I want to know how he's doing."

"You're leaving so soon?" A gaping sense of loss swallowed any relief she might have felt at the news.

"Yes," he said, "but before you start dancing on the ceiling to celebrate, don't take that to mean I'm walking out on my son. Here is what is going to happen. First, I'm going to set up a trust fund for him."

"Michael, that really isn't necessary. I have money enough to support him."

"I don't care what you have. It's what Kay has to give that matters here. Sooner or later, he's going to ask about his birth mother—what she was like, why she gave him up. For his sake, I intend to paint as positive a picture as possible. For him to learn the uglier aspects of his adoption can only hurt him."

"I agree," she said. "And if that's all you meant by your promise to take care of him, I can certainly live with it."

"Oh, there's more," he informed her, with the same brutal candor. "I intend to phone every Sunday evening before he goes to bed. You will see to it that he's available to take my calls uninterrupted by anyone else, most particularly your parents. He and I will talk for as long as it pleases us, and you will not listen in because you have my word that nothing I say will in any way disturb or confuse him. To all intents and purposes, I will remain for now the family friend he met for the first time this summer. *For now,* Camille.''

Although he'd said nothing which directly threatened her custodial rights, the implication that the worst was yet to come left her palms slippery with sweat. ''And later?''

''That's where you come in, my dear. You are going to tell him I'm his father. Exactly how you go about that is up to you, although I strongly suggest you exercise due caution, and control any inclination you might have to portray me as the villain of the piece. If that means putting a gag order on your parents, do that as well, because I won't tolerate their negative input.''

''I see,'' she said, the chill emanating from the telephone invading her bones. ''Have you also circled the date when all this is to occur?''

''I'm prepared to be flexible on that. You have until the beginning of December to get him used to the idea that he has a father with whom he'll be spending his birthday and Christmas.''

''You expect me to let you take him to Canada for Christmas?''

''Not this year. We'll start out with small changes. I'll come to California on both occasions. But I *will* see him every day that I'm there. I'll watch him blow out his birthday candles. At Christmas, I'll take him to see the sights, we'll go shopping together to buy a tree, I'll be the one to set it up and help him hang his stocking. And I'll be there Christmas morning when it's time to open gifts. I've missed playing Santa Claus for his first three years. I'm not about to be shut out of the fourth.''

''But what about us, Michael?'' she said.

"We'll be civil to one another," he told her, misunderstanding, deliberately or otherwise, what she was really asking. "I'll give you a bottle of perfume, you can buy me a pair of socks—we'll go through all the proper festive motions. But there is no 'us'. We're not even friends, Camille. Not anymore. But because we both care about Jeremy, we'll put on a convincing show."

"I'm not sure that I can do that," she said, her heart breaking.

"Then go spend Christmas and his birthday with your parents. But don't even think about inviting them over to your place or I'll take Jeremy somewhere else both days."

"Is this all I have to look forward from now on—just one ultimatum after another, or else?"

"More or less. When he's a bit older, we'll arrange to share holiday visits. You'll put him on a plane for the two-hour flight to Vancouver, and I'll be there at the other end to meet him. Divorced couples do that all the time and it seems to work well enough."

"We aren't divorced."

"No. And never will be because—"

"Because we'll never be married. I already know that, Michael. You don't have to keep rubbing it in. I just wish we could have found a way—"

"Wishing isn't enough, Camille," he said, just the slightest hint of regret shading his tone. "We've got too many things going against us and we both know cobbling together a marriage for Jeremy's sake does him no favors at all if, in the end, it blows up in his face. And it would, because although you might be ready to—how did you so charmingly put it? *Sell your soul to the devil if you had to?*—I'm not interested in buying."

"You're never going to forgive me for that, are you?"

"I already have, sweet thing. It's part of the past—just like you."

"So why keep bringing it up?"

"Because it showed a side of you I could never live with, no matter what perks might come with such an arrangement. Marriage is an adult undertaking, Camille, and I realized this afternoon that, at heart, you're still just a spoiled little girl playing with her doll and all her other fancy toys. If you ever decide to grow up, give me a call and we'll see where things go. In the meantime, I'll have my lawyers draw up a binding agreement for visitation rights."

There was a click and the line went dead. Phone in hand, she stared at the luxury surrounding her: the thick Chinese rugs, the white lacquered baby grand piano, the original oil paintings on the silk-paneled walls, and the plump cushioned sofas upholstered in fabric imported from France. And for the first time in her life, she felt poor. Because he was right. She was a thirty-year-old juvenile posing as a woman, and she was pathetic. *Pathetic!*

But she was a fighter, too. And he'd left the door to the future open just a crack. It wasn't much on which to pin her hopes, but it was enough. She'd show him she was worth a second chance!

"Are you telling me you'd proposed to the man and he was considering accepting, but you let him wriggle off the hook, and here you are, nearly a month later, and you've done nothing to try to lure him back?" Fran didn't bother to contain her disgust. "Honestly, Camille, you deserve all the grief you get! Why in heaven's name didn't you tell your parents to put a sock in it and show them the door, instead of wasting your breath attempting to justify something so far beyond their understanding that if you try for the next fifty years, you'll never convince them you're capable of making your own decisions?''

''I realize I didn't handle things well.''

''Obviously you don't, or you'd have done something about it by now.''

''I have. That is, I've come up with a plan.'' Camille ran her finger over the rim of her teacup, debating how to broach the subject which had brought her to the Knowlton house at a time when she'd normally have been reading Jeremy a bedtime story.

''Sitting here confiding your misery to me doesn't count,'' Fran told her. ''I'm not the one you have to convince to give you a second chance, Michael is.''

''I know, but I hardly expect him to believe in an overnight miracle. He's been gone only a month, Fran.''

''Do you love the guy?''

''Oh…!'' She scrunched her eyes shut and bit her lip against the sharp ache of missing him which stalked her night and day. ''*Yes,* I love him!''

''So tell him so.''

''I can't. Not yet.''

''Why not? I'd have thought, given that you've had it up to your ears with subterfuge and lies, that the truth might be an attractive option for a change.''

''I don't want him to think I'm desperate.''

''Why would he, when you've gone along with everything he's asked for regarding access to Jeremy?''

''Because I'm pregnant.''

There, the suspicion she'd harbored for over a week, and which a doctor in the city had confirmed that afternoon, was out! ''It's true,'' she said, laughing despite herself at the stunned expression on her friend's face. ''I'm going to have a baby.''

''*A* baby?'' Fran echoed. ''How about *his* baby?''

"Of course *his* baby! I'm insulted you'd think otherwise."

"No, you're not," Fran said. "You're so pleased with yourself you can hardly sit still. When are you going to tell him?"

"Not until I've cleaned up the mess I made of everything before he left."

"Hmm. Probably a wise choice. Because of course, once he knows he's going to be a father again, he'll marry you regardless and that's not good enough, is it?"

"No," she said. "It has to be because he believes in me."

"Does anyone else know you're pregnant?"

"If you mean, have I told my parents, no, I haven't. Michael deserves to hear before they do. I wouldn't have told you, Fran, except that…well, I had to tell someone, or I'd have burst!"

"I guess!" Fran came to sit beside her on the sofa and hugged her. "Imagine, after all those years of trying and not succeeding, you got pregnant just like that! Who'd have thought it?"

"I know." She folded her hands over her womb. "And we only did it twice!"

Fran collapsed into giggles. "With a guy like Michael, once was probably enough!" Then, sobering, she said, "So, what comes next?"

"I want to hold off saying anything to him until I'm past the first trimester because I don't know that he could weather the disappointment if I were to miscarry."

"You're not going to miscarry," Fran said firmly. "You're going to sail through this pregnancy without any problems and present him with a beautiful new son or daughter, and you're all going to live happily ever after."

"I hope so. But there's also something else. I have to

tell Jeremy that Michael's his father. It's the only way I can prove I'm living up to my side of the agreement. But I think it's important to give them enough time to cement their relationship through their weekly phone calls before I say anything.''

''Although you're probably right, I feel compelled to point out that if you put it off too long, you won't have to worry about telling your parents or anyone else around here that you're expecting. They'll be able to see it for themselves.''

''I know. So I thought I'd fly up to Vancouver around the end of October. I'll be almost eighteen weeks along by then.''

''And definitely pushing your luck!''

''It can't be helped. I'll just have to wear loose clothes and stay out of the pool when anyone's around.''

But that would be easy compared to the patience she'd need to see her through the eleven weeks before she'd see him again.

CHAPTER ELEVEN

FALL came early that year, with a series of October wind storms and rain which pretty much matched Mike's uncertain temper. He'd thought throwing himself into the multimillion dollar town home project would take his mind off Camille. It hadn't.

He'd thought strengthening his ties to his son would make up for his failed relationship with her. It didn't. If anything, hearing her answer the phone when he made his Sunday calls intensified the wrenching sense of loss he couldn't shake, no matter how many times he told himself he was better off without her.

He had to curb the urge to try to engage her in conversation, but she made that part easy by wasting no time putting Jeremy on the line. In fact, the sum total of her words to him each week were a nauseatingly cheerful, "Hello, Michael. Here's Jeremy."

The December deadline he'd given her was still over a month away, and how he was going to last that long without seeing her was reason enough to put a permanent scowl on his face. So when he arrived at the construction site on the morning of Friday the twenty-fifth and the first thing he learned was that some clown had put his steel-toed boot through the etched glass panel of an expensive front door, he was not disposed to be lenient.

Neither the man nor the boot was hurt, but the door was a write-off. Normally, he'd have chalked up the incident to the price of doing business, but that particular employee had been careless before and this latest episode was enough to send Mike into a towering rage. "You're a liability to yourself and everyone else on this site," he exploded. "Pull one more stunt like this, and you'll be history, you hear?"

"Half the neighborhood heard, boss," his foreman Doug Russell advised him as the man slunk off. "Including the prospective client who's been waiting over an hour to see you."

"I'm in no mood to speak to clients, prospective or otherwise. Refer him to the sales team."

"It's a 'her,' and I already went that route, but she's adamant. She wants you."

He cursed, something he was doing a lot of these days.

"Yeah," Doug cracked. "I tried telling her that as well, but she's not the type to take a hint."

"As if I don't have enough on my plate!" He stomped into the display unit and flung a tube of blueprints on the granite kitchen counter. "All right, let's get it over with. Where is she?"

"Last I saw, she was wandering around the Greenwood model."

"What?" He thumped his fist on the counter. "Has everyone around here gone nuts? That's a hard-hat area and you of all people know what'll happen if she trips over a ladder and breaks an ankle! I'll be up to my keister in a lawsuit I don't need."

"No, you won't, and please don't take out your annoyance on Mr. Russell. He warned me of the danger and I assured him I wouldn't hold anyone to blame if I got hurt."

That voice…he'd heard it in his dreams so often of late that at first he thought it was just his imagination playing another cruel trick on him. But when he wheeled around, there she was in the flesh, stepping in her dainty little boots over the roll of carpet blocking the foyer, and looking totally absurd in a bright yellow hard hat which clashed horribly with her rose pink raincoat.

"Uh...." he grunted, giving a fair imitation of a trained ape having a tough time deciding which banana he wanted for lunch.

By contrast, she was the epitome of calm self-assurance. "Is there someplace we can talk privately, Michael?"

He snapped his mouth shut before he grunted again, and tried to look intelligent.

"I'll make myself scarce, *Michael!*" Doug snickered.

She bathed him in a smile. "Oh, please, Mr. Russell, don't let me chase you away."

"*Go!*" Mike muttered, jabbing him in the ribs with his elbow.

With a last knowing smirk, Doug clumped out. Desperate to fill the cavernous silence he left behind, Mike said, "Is something wrong with Jeremy? Is that what's brought you here?"

He came across like a prison warden who hated his job, but if she noticed his tone was less than welcoming, she gave no indication. She picked her way past a pile of drop cloths the painters had dumped in the middle of the kitchen floor, and went to inspect the built-in china closet in the butler's pantry.

"Jeremy's perfectly fine. Growing like a weed, of course, but that's to be expected."

"Then why? And don't bother giving me the line about being a prospective client because I'm not buying it."

"If I *were* in the market for a town house, I'd certainly be interested in what you're offering here. This is lovely, Michael." She ran an appraising finger over the felt-lined silverware drawer then, when he was just about ready to rap his knuckles on her hard hat and force her to give him a straight answer, turned and said, "I have some rather momentous news, and I wanted to give it to you in person."

His stomach lurched and came to rest somewhere in the vicinity of his knees. Cripes, she'd met someone! She was getting married again to some blue-chip Californian, he just knew it! "I see," he said, sounding as if he'd got a three-inch rusty nail lodged in his windpipe. "Well? I'm listening."

"Not here, Michael. Isn't there a coffee shop close by, where we can talk without being overheard?"

"No," he said. "The nearest one is a ten minute drive away in Crescent Beach and I can't see you being comfortable in a pickup truck."

"As long as you do the driving, it won't be a problem."

"I'm a busy man. Time's money, and I can't afford to waste it."

She shifted the bag slung over her shoulder and marched across the floor to trap him between her and the kitchen island. "I'm asking for half an hour, Michael. You can spare me that, surely?"

Hell, he might as well get it over with! "Okay. My truck's in the driveway."

"I know," she said. "I saw you drive up. Dark blue with a gray stripe, right?"

"Right. Not quite the deluxe transportation you're used to, is it?"

"A lot of things I'm not used to have happened to me since I saw you last," she said cryptically, setting her hard hat on the counter, "and I don't mind admitting I'm finding the changes rather refreshing."

The fragrance of her shampoo, mingling with the smell of new paint and freshly sawn wood, formed a powerful aphrodisiac. Before he did something stupid, like pulling her into his arms, he jammed his hands in the pockets of his jean jacket and brushed past her. "I bet! Well, let's get moving. I don't have all day."

The coffee shop was half empty and they were able to seclude themselves in a booth near the back. "No thanks," she said, when he asked her if she wanted anything to eat with her coffee. "And I'd prefer tea. Lapsang souchong, if they have it."

Not everything about you has changed, sweetheart, he thought, burying a grin. "Camille, this is a mom-and-pop café, not the Ritz-Carlton. I doubt the couple who run the joint have ever heard of Lapsang souchong."

She blushed and he realized how much he'd missed seeing her do that. As much as he'd missed looking at her...kissing her...making love to her and feeling her clench around him just before she came. "Of course. What was I thinking? I'll just have tea, please."

What the hell was *he* thinking! Cripes, he was as hard as a rock! "Okay, what's so important that you had to come all the way up here to tell me about it?" he asked brusquely, once their tea and coffee had arrived.

"I'm planning to leave California. To leave the U.S. altogether, as a matter of fact."

It was even worse than he'd first thought. She was marrying some guy who lived in northern Tibet or some other far-flung spot on the map, and he'd never see her again. "Why?"

"Well, I'm hoping to get married."

He wasn't hard anymore. Hearing her confirm his worst fear left him feeling as if someone had swung a mallet at his delicate parts.

Even though he usually drank it straight, he made a big production of pouring sugar into his coffee because he couldn't bring himself to look at her. "Kind of a sudden decision, isn't it?"

"Not really."

He tipped another spoonful of sugar into his mug. "How do he and Jeremy get along?"

"Famously. Just like father and son."

The canister slipped out of his hand and sent a spray of sugar skittering across the fake wood tabletop. "In case you've forgotten, Camille," he said, barely able to control the fury and jealousy roaring through him, "Jeremy already has a father."

"I know, Michael," she said, not sounding nearly as sure of herself as she had before. "And I'm rather hoping, if I ask very nicely this time, that he'll agree to make an honest woman of me."

"Huh?" Sad to say, he was back to the trained ape bit again, but his brain was too busy scrambling to make sense of what she'd just said to come up with much in the way of witty repartee.

She leaned on the table and sent another drift of shampoo and perfume floating toward him. "You turned me down the last time I proposed, because you said, quite rightly, that I needed to grow up. Well, I've tried hard to do that in the months since you left and I hope, when you hear of the changes I've made, that you'll reconsider your decision."

He cut her off with a slash of his hand. "Hold on a minute and let me be sure I've got this straight."

She sat very erect and folded her hands primly in her lap. Her face was blindingly beautiful, from the radiant bloom of her skin to her huge, serious eyes and sweetly compressed mouth. Her hair, even on a day as gray as this, gleamed like spun gold caught in the rays of an April sunrise.

"You came all this way to propose?"

She nodded.

"It couldn't have waited until Christmas?"

She shook her head.

He leaned back in the booth and stared at the ceiling, the No Smoking sign, the plastic roses in a vase on the glass-fronted display case in the corner—*anywhere* but at her. "Well, it's something to consider, I suppose."

"I won't ask if that's a yes," she said, finding her tongue again, "because I don't want your answer yet."

He shot her a glance from beneath his lashes. "Setting out conditions already, Camille?"

"Just one." She clasped her hands earnestly. "I want you to hear me out and then take the rest of the day to mull over what I've said, before you make up your mind. I've given this a great deal of thought, Michael, and it wouldn't be fair of me to expect you to commit one way or the other until you've had time to digest the pros and cons."

"Name some of the cons."

She lifted one shoulder in a tiny shrug. "I'm used to being a single parent and having the final say on how I want things done. It might take a while for me to 'get used to sharing my toys', as you once put it—although I hasten to add that I've never regarded Jeremy as a toy. Also, I'm very well off, and I don't know how you'll handle that. Some men find it difficult having a rich wife." She lowered her eyes and hesitated before finishing, "And last, it's possible you're involved with someone else."

"And the pros?"

"It would be wonderful for Jeremy to have two parents living under the same roof, and I'd do my very best never to make you regret being my husband."

"Is that all, Camille?" he goaded her. "You can't think of a more *intimate* reason for us to tie the knot?"

She blushed again and refused to meet his gaze. "Well, we are…compatible."

"Compatible how?"

She bit her lip, but couldn't stop the smile tugging at her mouth. "You know! Sex."

"Ah, yes," he said. "Sex. I'd hate to overlook *that* as I weigh my options."

"But there's more, Michael," she said, sobering. "I want you to know that no matter what you decide, I do intend to leave California, and I am resolved to move here. I've looked into it, and because Jeremy has a Canadian father, that won't be a problem with the authorities."

It was a shame that he had to prick such a tantalizing bubble of fantasy, but the probable obstacles weren't something he could ignore, even if she could. "And what do your parents have to say about all this?"

"They don't know yet."

"Aha! Enter major stumbling block number one! Once they find out, they'll never let you get away with it."

"It isn't up to them," she said flatly. "This is my decision. Jeremy's the one who needs to live close to both his parents, not I. And as you so succinctly pointed out, it's long past time I severed the apron strings with my mother and father. I love them, but I don't need them telling me how to run my life and I'm afraid they're going to have to accept that."

He made a tunnel with his hands and blew down it. "You'll find it's easier said than done. When you actually get right down to—"

"I've already sold my house, Michael. The new owners take possession at the end of November. You might turn me down, but you're not going to get rid of me. I'll look for a place near where you live so that Jeremy can visit you every day. Next door, if I can swing it!"

"Whew!" He shook his head. "Talk about tearing up roots and starting over in a big way!"

"Well, it's time I showed a little backbone, don't you think? And you must admit it'll simplify everything if we're close by. Next year, Jeremy will start school. Before long, he'll want to play soccer and basketball and all those other boy things that I know nothing about. And he'll want his daddy to be there to coach him and cheer him on."

Touched more than he cared to admit, he said, "You don't have to sell me on fatherhood, Camille."

"I know," she said. "But I am hoping I can sell you on marriage. I'm hoping you'll believe me when I say that I would be honored to be your wife, but if you decide to turn me down, I'm not going to pack up my toys and go running back home to sulk. I've grown up enough to handle disappointment without falling apart, Michael."

"Let me get back to you later," he said, afraid if he didn't shut her up, he'd lose it and start bawling. She was offering him the world—and talking as if he'd be doing her a favor by accepting it. It was more than he'd dared hope for; more than he deserved. "Where are you staying?"

"At the Pan Pacific. I wondered, if you don't have other plans, if you'd like to meet me there for dinner tonight?"

"Yeah," he said. "I'd like that very much."

"Then I'll make a reservation as soon as I get back. Is seven too early?"

"Uh-uh. Seven's fine." He pulled back his sleeve and checked his watch. "Look, I really have to get back to the job site. I'm expecting building inspectors in another twenty minutes."

She swept up her bag and slithered out from the booth. "I understand. Thank you for taking the time to meet with me."

"You're welcome."

He followed her out to the sidewalk and unlocked the truck. She smiled and thanked him as he helped her into the passenger seat. He said "You're welcome," again, went around to the driver's door, and climbed in.

"This is a very comfortable vehicle," she said.

"Yeah," he said, rolling his eyes and wondering how he could tactfully put an end to an exchange growing more stilted by the minute. But it was a delicate situation. She'd put her pride on the line and he'd been caught by surprise. It wouldn't do to rush things. They were talking big decisions here—decisions that would affect the rest of their lives, and Jeremy's, too. They both needed to be sure they understood exactly what they were getting themselves into because once done, there'd be no undoing it.

She perched in her seat, her pink raincoat wrapped around her, her outsize bag clutched in her lap, her eyes on the road ahead. "Oh, look!" she exclaimed, with painfully manufactured enthusiasm, as he turned the truck around and headed back the way they'd come. "A train!"

She'd been spending so much time with a three-year-old, she was starting to sound like one. And he wasn't much better, hedging his bets and dithering like somebody's maiden aunt. Caution be damned!

He cruised to a stop a yard or so short of the level crossing. "Yeah," he said again, cupping his hand around her neck and weaving his fingers through her silky hair. "A train. And just in the nick of time, too. It saves me having to find a place to park and do this."

He pulled her toward him and she didn't resist. She leaned across the console, her mouth trembling, her eyes glassy with tears, and lifted her face to his. Heart nearly bursting with pent-up emotion, he bent his head and kissed her. Then he kissed her again. And all the stress and tension he'd been carrying around for weeks flew out the window along with caution, and got swept away on the southwest gale thundering across the bay.

"Oh, thank you!" she whispered, when he stopped to let them both draw breath. "I'd just about given up hope that you were ever going to do that again."

"You might have come a long way since the last time we were together," he told her thickly, shaping the curve of her lip with his thumb, "but, honey, you've still got miles to go if you couldn't figure out I've been itching to kiss you from the minute I saw you modeling that hard hat."

She was at the table by a quarter to seven, just to be sure she'd be seated before he arrived. "He'll never suspect," Nori had assured her, when she'd asked if the peacock blue outfit made her look pregnant.

She sipped from her water glass. Rearranged the accordion pleats flowing from the nipped-in empire waist of her dress, and wondered if the fluttering in the pit of her stomach was the baby making its first tentative moves, or just sheer nerves.

The wall of windows next to the table showed the glimmering outline of watercraft bobbing at anchor in the harbor, and beyond, above the lantern-chain draping the hills on the other side of the Lion's Gate Bridge, the misty aura of floodlights piercing the rain clouds hanging over a mountain where, when the snow came, people could ski at night.

Superimposed over the spectacle, the reflection of the room behind her was flung back in perfect reproduction. The flash of silver caught her attention, the flicker of candles, and then, rising above the small crowd waiting to be seated, Michael's tall figure coming toward her.

Briefly, she closed her eyes and crossed her fingers. *Let it be a perfect evening!*

He bent over the back of her chair. Dropped a kiss on the crown of her head. "Am I late?"

"No," she said, savoring the sight of him all freshly shaved and sparkling in a navy suit and white shirt, with a burgundy silk tie. "I'm early."

"You look lovely, as always."

"So do you."

"Me, lovely?" He laughed and took a seat across from her. "That's a first—but then, there've been a number of those today." He raised his brows and gestured. "Are you expecting…?"

Her eyes flew wide in shock. She gulped and tried to stem the flush of guilt sweeping up from her feet to envelop her entire body. *He'd noticed!*

"…someone else to join us? I see we're at a table for three."

"Oh!" Relief gusted from her lungs and set the candle flame in the middle of the table to flickering. "Well, yes. Just for a short while."

Right on cue, Nori came into the restaurant with Jeremy, adorable in dark blue corduroy vest and pants, and a red striped shirt, at her side. He'd been so proud of his clothes, so excited about his part in the evening. Now, though, he was dragging his feet and looked ready to turn tail and run.

Camille knew how he felt. She was on pins and needles herself.

"Anyone I know?" Michael asked.

She nodded. "Mmm-hmm."

He inclined a taut smile her way. "Are we playing twenty questions, Camille?"

"No," she said, and held out her hand.

Jeremy ran the last few yards and flung himself at her, all the time peeking out at Michael whose face was a study. For once in his life, he was speechless.

Prying Jeremy loose, she steered him toward his father. "Go on, darling. Don't be shy. You know what to say."

"Hello, Daddy."

His voice might have been tentative as the cheep of a newly hatched bird, but there was no mistaking his words, or their effect on Michael.

He bounced his fist against his mouth, blinked, and stared fixedly out the window a moment. He cleared his throat once or twice, shook his head as if to dispel ideas too baffling and wonderful to be real then, when he'd wrestled himself under control, looked back at Jeremy and said gravely, "Hello, son."

Because she knew, if she gave in to the tears pressing behind her eyeballs, that Jeremy would start crying, too, Camille buried her nose in her glass and drained half the ice water in one go.

When she dared to look up again, she found Michael watching her from eyes turned nearly purple with emotion. "You," he murmured, "are one tough act to follow."

"I'm not trying to bribe you, you know. There are no strings attached to what just happened."

"Oh, there are strings, Camille, and they're wrapped so tight around my heart it's barely managing to function."

Jeremy leaned against his knee. "Now that you're my daddy, are you coming to live at our house?"

"Er...no, son."

"Can we come to yours?"

Before Michael could answer, Camille said, "Remember what I told you this afternoon, Jeremy, when we went to the aquarium? That if we couldn't live with daddy, we'd live near him? And after, when we went for a drive, remember those lovely houses by the sea that you liked so much?"

He nodded and fixed his attention on Michael again. "Is that where you live?"

"No," Michael said. "I live in an apartment, but I've been thinking I wouldn't mind living by the sea, in a house with a big garden where a boy and his daddy could kick a ball around."

"With a dog, right?"

"A dog sounds like a fine idea to me."

"And I could bring my racing car and drive all over the garden?"

"Sure."

"And Mommy can come, too?"

Michael's gaze met hers. "Oh, yes. Mommy is definitely part of the deal."

Jeremy heaved a sigh of contentment. "I think I'll like living here."

"And I think this calls for champagne." Michael signaled the waiter. "It's not every day a man gets to have dinner with his son."

He ordered sparkling apple juice served in champagne flutes. "To the future," he said, raising his glass. "And to the three of us."

"Cheers!" Jeremy piped up, clearly delighted with all the pomp and ceremony.

It was just as well Nori came to collect him a short time later, before the excitement became too much for him.

He watched as his son trotted off with the nanny, then swung back to face her. "I never thought I'd say this but, just this once, I'm glad to see him leave. Because you and I have business to discuss."

"Oh dear!" She dabbed the corner of her mouth with her napkin. "That sounds ominous."

"First, I have to tell you I've never seen you look more

beautiful. You're glowing, Camille, in a way you never were before. You light up this entire room.''

''I'm happy.'' She lowered her eyes almost shyly. ''Happy to be here. Happy to be with you.''

''Me, too. And it's been a long time since I've been able to say that.'' He reached into his inside pocket and took out the velvet bag he'd stashed there. ''I thought, when I went shopping for a ring this afternoon, that giving it to you would be the highlight of the evening, but you upstaged me with Jeremy. Nothing will ever equal that. But at least you know the reason I'm accepting your proposal has nothing to do with what you've given me tonight.''

She gasped a little and covered her mouth with both hands. Her eyes were big as saucers and suspiciously bright. ''Oh, Michael, that's the nicest thing you've ever said to me!''

''But telling you I love you is the most important. I can't promise I'll always be nice because I'm not always a very nice person, but I swear to you, I'll love you for the rest of my life.''

A tear fell down her face, bright as a shooting star. ''You don't have to say that, you know.''

''I wouldn't, if I didn't mean it. 'I love you' aren't words I toss around lightly. So believe me when I say, I do love you. Very much.''

She sniffed, and still managed to look beautiful. ''I wanted to be the first to say that to you. Because I love you, too, with all my heart.''

''Too bad, spoilt little rich girl,'' he said. ''I beat you to it and I'm never going to let you forget it.'' He loosened the cord at the neck of the bag and tipped the ring into the palm of his hand. ''Will wearing this help you get over the disappointment?''

He took the third finger of her left hand and slipped the

ring into place. It was at least two sizes too big, but the diamond solitaire was perfect. Elegant and classic and matchless, just like her. "If you don't like it, we can return it and choose something else."

"I absolutely love it," she cried softly, and patted the chair next to hers. "Come and sit beside me, Michael. I have something to give to you, too."

He didn't need to be asked twice. He'd been waiting all night to get close to her. But, "I've already got more than any man could want," he said. "I've got you and Jeremy. I don't need anything else."

"Oh, I hope you don't mean that." Her smile, shining through the tears, was tremulous. "Because this is *not* something that can be returned or exchanged."

She took his hand and placed it at her waist. At least, it used to be her waist. But underneath the yards of silk, or whatever her dress was made of, he felt something round and solid. Like a little football. Or a basketball.

He snatched his hand away and jumped up from the table. "What have you got hidden under there, Camille?"

"I'm not sure yet," she said demurely. "It's either a boy or a girl. Congratulations, Michael. You're going to be a daddy again."

He didn't know how it felt to pass out, but the dizzying pattern of black dots dancing before his eyes suggested he might be about to find out. Slumping back into the chair, he eyed her nervously. Now that he knew what to look for, the basketball was pretty hard to miss. "Are you telling me you're pregnant?"

She let out a giggle, something he hated in other women but which rippled out of her mouth like music. "Oh, I hope so, otherwise I'm in trouble."

"You're in trouble anyway, you little witch," he

growled. ''Why didn't you say something sooner? What if I'd refused to see you? What if I'd turned you down?''

''That's precisely why I didn't tell you. I didn't want you marrying me out of obligation or pity.''

His mouth dropped open. ''You know what? You're daft!''

''I'm carrying your baby, as well,'' she said, bold as brass. ''So watch your language.''

He started shaking with laughter. His mouth split in a mile-wide grin. Grabbing her by the shoulders, he planted a kiss full on her lips and didn't give a rap who saw. ''Forget dinner,'' he said against her mouth. ''You're coming with me. This baby and I need to get better acquainted.''

He rented a suite overlooking the water. He told her he loved her, that he'd loved her for a long time. He took off all her clothes and laid his face on her bare stomach and told his baby he loved it, too. He held her in his arms and kissed away the happy tears she shed.

And finally, with the moon peeping through the window from between ragged clouds, he made love to her.

In a bed.

At last.

Modern Romance™
...seduction and
passion guaranteed

Tender Romance™
...love affairs that
last a lifetime

Sensual Romance™
...sassy, sexy and
seductive

Blaze™
...sultry days and
steamy nights

Medical Romance™
...medical drama on
the pulse

Historical Romance™
...rich, vivid and
passionate

29 new titles every month.

*With all kinds of Romance for
every kind of mood...*

MILLS & BOON®

Makes any time special™

MAT4

MILLS & BOON®

Modern Romance™

SOCIETY WEDDINGS BY KENDRICK & WALKER

PROMISED TO THE SHEIKH *by Sharon Kendrick*

The only way Jenna can get out of the wedding to
Sheikh Rashid of Quador is to pretend she is no longer
a virgin, but what happens when sizzling attraction
overwhelms them and Rashid discovers she's lying?

THE DUKE'S SECRET WIFE *by Kate Walker*

Just when Isabelle thinks their secret marriage is over,
Don Luis de Silva, heir to the dukedom of Madrigal,
asks her to return to Spain. But what does Luis have
to gain from this reunion?

RYAN'S REVENGE *by Lee Wilkinson*

Jilted at the altar. No one can do that to Ryan Falconer
and get away with it. That's why, two years later, Ryan's
back, convinced their passionate love isn't d ead. He's
determined to lead Virginia down the aisle – willing or not!

HER DETERMINED HUSBAND *by Kathryn Ross*

Kirsten discovers she must work intimately with Cal
McCormick, her estranged husband! Only a few years
before, tragedy had ripped apart their young marriage,
but now Cal seems set on making her fall in love with
him all over again...

THE RUNAWAY PRINCESS *by Patricia Forsythe*

Marriage to a man who would love her was Alexis's
most cherished dream. But how would Jace react
when he discovered the truth about her? That the
beautiful substitute teacher was actually a princess...

On sale 1st March 2002

*Available at most branches of WH Smith,
Tesco, Martins, Borders, Eason, Sainsbury's
and most good paperback bookshops.*
0202/01b

Treat yourself this Mother's Day to the ultimate indulgence

3 brand new romance novels and a box of chocolates

= *only £7.99*

Available from 15th February

MIRANDA LEE

Secrets & Sins *revealed*

SEDUCED BY HER BODYGUARD AND STALKED BY A STRANGER...

Available from 15th March 2002

*Available at most branches of WH Smith,
Tesco, Martins, Borders, Eason, Sainsbury's
and most good paperback bookshops.*

0402/35/MB34

Starting Over

Another chance at love...
Found where least expected

PENNY JORDAN

Published 15th February

Available at most branches of WH Smith,
Tesco, Martins, Borders, Eason, Sainsbury's
and most good paperback bookshops.

FREE!

2 Books
and a surprise gift!

We would like to take this opportunity to thank you for reading this Mills & Boon® book by offering you the chance to take TWO more specially selected titles from the Modern Romance™ series absolutely FREE! We're also making this offer to introduce you to the benefits of the Reader Service™—

- ★ FREE home delivery
- ★ FREE gifts and competitions
- ★ FREE monthly Newsletter
- ★ Books available before they're in the shops
- ★ Exclusive Reader Service discount

Accepting these FREE books and gift places you under no obligation to buy; you may cancel at any time, even after receiving your free shipment. Simply complete your details below and return the entire page to the address below. *You don't even need a stamp!*

YES! Please send me 2 free Modern Romance books and a surprise gift. I understand that unless you hear from me, I will receive 4 superb new titles every month for just £2.49 each, postage and packing free. I am under no obligation to purchase any books and may cancel my subscription at any time. The free books and gift will be mine to keep in any case.

P2ZEB

Ms/Mrs/Miss/Mr ....Initials..................................
BLOCK CAPITALS PLEASE

Surname...

Address..

....

....Postcode ....

Send this whole page to:
UK: The Reader Service, FREEPOST CN81, Croydon, CR9 3WZ
EIRE: The Reader Service, PO Box 4546, Kilcock, County Kildare (stamp required)